the puberty Game

a guide to help parents get ready to play

the puberty Game

a guide to help parents get ready to play

John Court

HarperCollins*Publishers*

All the case notes quoted in this book are based on the author's experience, but details are so changed that anyone who may think that they can identify themselves or someone they know will almost certainly be wrong.

HarperCollins*Publishers*
First published in Australia in 1997
by HarperCollinsPublishers Pty Limited
ACN 009 913 517

A member of the HarperCollins*Publishers* (Australia) Pty Limited Group
Copyright © 1997 John Court

HarperCollins*Publishers*
25 Ryde Road, Pymble, Sydney NSW 2073, Australia
31 View Road, Glenfield, Auckland 10, New Zealand
77–85 Fulham Palace Road, London W6 8JB, United Kingdom
Hazelton Lanes, 55 Avenue Road, Suite 2900, Toronto, Ontario, M5R 3L2
and 1995 Markham Road, Scarborough, Ontario M1B 5M8, Canada
10 East 53rd Street, New York NY 10032, USA

The National Library of Australia Cataloguing-in-Publication data:
 Court, John M, (John Maurice), 1929-
 The puberty game: a guide to help parents ready to play.

 Includes index.
 ISBN 0 7 322 578 67
 1. Teenagers. 2. Parent and teenager. 1. Title
649.125
Cover illustration by Scott Rigney

Printed in Australia by Griffin Paperbacks.
9 8 7 6 5 4 3 2 1
99 98 97

C o n t e n t s

Contents

Foreword

I often think of the whole process of adolescence as being very similar to a roller coaster ride, on which parents buy a ticket when their children turn eleven or twelve. As many parents discover, there is no getting off this ride until it is over and increasing numbers of parents, instead of enjoying the exhilaration from childhood to adulthood, spend this time white-knuckled with fear as they cling to the side of the roller coaster, hoping not to fall out.

Parents in the late 1990s face a singular challenge, as not only are young people reaching puberty earlier than ever before, they are simultaneously drowning in an information explosion that is unique to our time. While we have created a generation of young people who on the one hand have never been told so much, on the other hand never have they known so little, as wisdom is very thin on the ground. In many instances their alleged 'street wisdom' is nothing more than a veneer over an aching void of uncertainty, confusion and self-doubt. It could be argued that no set of parents in history have needed the skills to understand and communicate with their teenagers more than today's.

In writing *The puberty game*, one of Australia's most eminent adolescent physicians has provided today's parents and care givers with a clear and simple 'map' of this roller coaster ride. This book is replete with explicit instructions designed to assist parents experience the various twists and turns that this roller coaster takes and to help guide them over unfamiliar emotional terrain.

John Court has shown the reader that the early adolescent is caught between a lost childhood and an unrealised adulthood, trying to cope with new types of friendships, burgeoning sexuality, changing interests and a beginning awareness of self. It is a time of transition from a place in the family to a place in the outside world, a time of great anxiety, apprehension, expectation of the fear and thrill of the unknown.

Most importantly, it is a time when physical growth is occurring more rapidly than at any other stage, except in the womb, and when alongside that changes in mental and emotional growth are most insistent and demanding. John Court shows that these changes are equally full of conflict and challenging to parents attempting to understand them, as they are to the young person themselves - torn between wanting and not wanting to be understood.

This is arguably one of the most vulnerable generations in history and caring for teenagers has never been so complex a task. *The puberty game* comprehensively fills a longstanding void in parent education literature and is written with the understanding and compassion you would expect from one of Australia's leading adolescent specialists. If you are looking for a practical, no-nonsense book on early adolescence with straightforward advice that is logical and fair, look no further...

Michael Carr-Gregg PhD
Head
Education Unit
Centre for Adolescent Health
Melbourne

About the author

Dr John Court is a paediatric physician specialising in adolescent health.

His principal interests are in the area of growth and adolescence, with particular concern for young people with chronic illness as they pass from childhood to adult life. He believes in the active involvement of young people in making decisions about programmes promoting adolescent health. He spends much of his time in schools and he is concerned with the ways in which physicians and teachers can cooperate with parents in helping teenagers with learning and behaviour problems.

Dr Court has spent most of his professional life in Australia, apart from periods of study and research in the UK. He has been a regular lecturer in Malaysia, Singapore, Hong Kong, China and Japan. He has been widely published in medical journals and books and for many years was the editor of *Australian Paediatric Journal* and the *Newsletter of the International Association of Adolescent Health*. He is currently editor-in-chief of the international *Journal of Pediatrics and Child Health*.

He was a Foundation Member, and later President, of the Australian Association for Adolescent Health. He developed a medical service for adolescents at Melbourne's Royal Children's Hospital, and this has since been incorporated into the Centre for Adolescent Health, where he is a senior physician.

His work with adolescents, particularly those with diabetes, was recognised in 1993 when he was awarded the Member of the Order of Australia.

Acknowledgments

Young people in their teens and pre-teens have been generous in sharing their experiences and problems with the author. Parents have been generous in entrustng the author with the care of their children.

This book is dedicated to them all, and especially to the author's family - Judy, Andrew and Madeleine.

Introduction

Surviving the teens before they start

You hear so much about the Terrible Teens – far worse than the Terrible Twos we always knew about, and as they are so much bigger and stronger, there seems to be much less that parents can do about them. You read about drugs, sex, school drop-outs, youth suicide and unemployment. How can anyone possibly protect children from all this? How can you prevent your teenage child from getting hurt in a society where there are so many traps for people at this difficult time of life?

In fact, most teenagers don't get into trouble. Most develop into healthy young adults of whom their parents are very proud. With family support and encouragement, most cope well with their school and social life during their teenage years and achieve their potential for a healthy and happy future life.

But some don't. And some give their parents a very hard time in the process of growing up. Parents may then ask themselves what they could have done to protect their teenagers from going wrong or having so much difficulty in their lives.

There are plenty of things that parents can do to protect their children from the perils of the teenage years. Many of these things are best started well in advance, before they reach adolescence and while they are close to their parents and most amenable to help.

Be prepared

Children in their pre-teenage years give many warnings if they are heading for trouble and give many opportunities for parents to help them. The trouble for some parents is that they may be preoccupied with their own problems. When children are getting older, families are often under the greatest stress with financial worries and marital difficulties. There are the pressures of balancing time between work and home, between fulfiling all the needs of each of the children and not neglecting those who seem to be most self-sufficient.

Despite these difficulties for parents, there are some things they can consider doing that do not need to take up much time and which will pay dividends in the following years.

Talk to your pre-teen about the things that are important to both of you

Now is the time to talk about things like sex, drugs, friends and growing up with increasing freedoms and responsibilities. Don't leave it until they are involved in the teen scene and decide that you probably don't know much or you wouldn't understand.

Make sure your child feels strong about themselves

This depends not only on their personal strengths and self-esteem, but on how they feel valued as a member of the family.

Make sure that your child feels they really belong to their family

There may be many times in the future that family ties will be challenged, and a strong feeling of connection to the family now will help withstand all sorts of threats from both within and without the family. The same applies to school and to their group of friends. The family is as vital to the health and happiness of a teenager as it is to younger children and the pre-teenager.

Make sure that any difficulties at school have been sorted out

Many children have learning difficulties and some enter secondary school without anyone really understanding these difficulties or trying to overcome them. A child with Attention Deficit Disorder that has not been recognised by their pre-teens may become increasingly frustrated by bad reports and gain a reputation for bad behaviour when they are in secondary school.

Make sure that family rules are in place

Teenagers tend to challenge rules, especially ones that have only recently been imposed. They are especially likely to test out those rules that have been made because of unsafe or stupid teenage behaviour (like drinking, smoking and staying out late).

Make sure household chores are established

It's good for children to help around the house, especially if both parents work, but as they grow older they seem to resent having to do household chores unless the chores have become an established routine.

Make sure that both parents work together in how they bring up their children

This is just as important if parents are separated — perhaps even more so. Teenagers are very good at taking advantage of differences in how parents feel about restrictions, punishments and responsibilities. It is not good for pre-teenagers to get away with manipulating their parents by playing on their different attitudes towards child raising.

It has been shown in American studies that teenagers who have a strong sense of belonging to their family develop a resilience that helps to withstand many of the hazards of teenage culture, and are less likely to be involved in the more dangerous behaviours of youth.

Puberty

Puberty: coming, ready or not

Sara had been referred to me because her mother felt that she had started puberty too early. She was ten and had already started breast development. 'Quite frankly, Doctor,' Sara's mum said, 'I'm worried that she isn't ready for puberty yet. She seems quite confused about the changes that are happening to her body and I'm sure that she wouldn't be able to cope with periods.'

I remarked that other girls in her grade at school would probably also have started puberty.

'Well maybe Doctor, but her brother is almost thirteen and he isn't showing any signs of starting. I happened to see him examining himself for pubic hair the other day, and he seemed quite disappointed that there's nothing showing yet. And Sara is growing so fast that Damien is worried that she is getting taller than him.'

Sara had certainly started puberty. She had breast buds, and some pubic hair, which her mother hadn't noticed before, was developing along her labia.

Sara was very embarrassed about any of the other girls finding out about it. 'I told the girls at school that I was seeing a doctor for a sore elbow.'

'Do you have a sore elbow?' I asked.

'Not really, but can you just check on it please, so I can tell my friends that you did?'

We decided to put a bandaid on an imaginary spot on her elbow, and Sara's mother and I discussed the implications of early puberty in girls, and what to expect.

Puberty is getting earlier and earlier

About a century ago, in most countries, puberty tended to start later than it does now, and often not until the teenage years. Since then it has been starting earlier and earlier, and now, in

Australia, many girls have had their first period before their thirteenth birthday, which is three or four years earlier than girls a century and a half ago. Boys are getting taller than their fathers, and girls are getting taller than their mothers. So, puberty is arriving earlier and children are getting more physically advanced with each generation.

There may be several reasons for this. Perhaps it has been due to better nutrition in childhood. We know that undernourished children, particularly in countries where there are food shortages, grow more slowly than well-nourished ones. Another possible explanation is that we are able to treat illnesses and infections so much better now, and prevent others through immunisation. We know that children with recurrent or chronic illness often grow less well than healthy children. There are strong genetic factors responsible for growth and the timing of puberty. There are probably genes that determine how tall children will grow; and perhaps the greater population movement and ease in travel this century has led to the 'tallness genes' spreading more widely in the community.

Sometimes early puberty can be an advantage; but it's often a disadvantage, because a child's emotional development doesn't always keep pace with their early physical and sexual development. Sometimes pre-teens just don't seem to be ready for puberty. Others can't wait for it to begin!

What sets puberty off?

The timing of puberty, both when it starts and how long it takes, varies quite a lot from one child to another. It is almost certainly under genetic control, but what exactly triggers it off is still uncertain. It is as if there is a sort of 'time clock' in every child's brain that sends signals to the body when it is time to start puberty. After that, it is all under the control of certain glands in the body, and these glands will determine how fast puberty proceeds, controlling each stage of growth and pubescent development. This 'time clock' is probably set long before the child is born, and is largely governed by inherited factors. However, it can be changed throughout childhood by events along the way, such as illness and nutrition.

Some time before any outward signs of puberty occur, a gland called the pituitary gland (which can be found in the head just beneath the brain) starts to send signals to the glands that are responsible for sexual development. These glands are the testes in boys, and the ovaries in girls. Other glands are also involved: they are called the adrenal glands. The signals sent out by the pituitary gland are the hormones that circulate in the bloodstream to reach the testes, ovaries and adrenal glands, and it is possible to detect these hormones in the blood long before any outward signs of puberty can be found.

The dreaded hormones of puberty

The hormones from the pituitary gland stimulate the sex glands to develop. They increase in size and become more mature, and eventually produce the sex hormones that lead to the outward signs of puberty and sexual maturity. The very first signs of puberty are an increase in the size of the testes in boys and the ovaries in girls. Along with these physical changes there are also increasing amounts of the sex hormones produced by the ovaries and the testes. These hormones play a central role in determining the development of puberty, not only in the physical and sexual development, but also in the social and emotional changes that accompany puberty.

As the male and female sex hormones are very different, and have different effects on the body, from now on the development in boys and girls will be different.

When does puberty
normally start?

There is a very wide range of when is 'normal', so it is generally better to think of when puberty *usually* starts and what the range of ages is for most girls or boys. Then we can consider what should be done if the start of puberty in a particular child falls outside this range. If a child starts puberty very early, it may still be quite normal (but unusual); but it is also possible that something has gone wrong with the timing of puberty.

Girls usually start puberty in
their pre-teens

Most girls will have started breast development by the age of thirteen. This means that 95% of girls will have done so, but it also means that 5% of girls will not have started breast development by that age. Of these girls, most will be perfectly normal, but a few will have some hormonal problem to account for their late pubescent development.

If a girl hasn't any signs of breast development by the start of her teenage years, and she is worried about it, it is perfectly reasonable to seek advice from your doctor. This advice would most often be reassuring, but it can be helpful to check for other causes of being a late starter.

A very early start for puberty can be worrying both to a girl and to her parents. Girls can be very embarrassed about their breast development when they feel that they are the only one in their class at school who has started to develop. Parents are often more worried about how their daughter will cope with menstrual periods when she is so young, and her friends are still hardly showing any signs of development. So when should parents be concerned about their child if puberty seems to be starting too early?

Some breast development is quite common in infancy, and may even persist for several years, disappearing by the age of six, and usually earlier. It is usually of no consequence. Apart from this, however, it is very unusual for a girl to have signs of breast development before the age of nine. The development of pubic hair before the age of nine cannot be considered as being normal, and should always be checked out by your family doctor.

Boys start later than girls

Boys usually start puberty later than girls, and on average may be about eighteen months behind them with the outward signs of puberty. Although many boys will be showing some development of pubic hair when they are twelve, many will not, and this is perfectly normal. As in girls, early signs of puberty may mean that there is an hormonal disturbance. If a boy shows signs of pubic hair or growth of his penis before he is ten it would be wise to have it checked out by your doctor.

Boys often cope well with early puberty

Most boys who develop puberty early seem to cope rather well. Unlike girls who develop earlier than their friends, boys often enjoy their early masculinity and are proud of it. They may feel rather superior to other boys, and be more likely to succeed at football or be more competitive in team sports. They are more likely to be chosen as class captain and be a leader in their final primary school year. Of course, some may not, and sometimes these boys and their families have difficulty in coping with the bad moods and the emotional storms that so often accompany puberty.

In boys, late development is much more common than it is in girls, and is often a source of worry and annoyance to them. This is hardly a concern for the pre-teenager, and is more a problem in the mid-teenage years.

(See You and your teenager, *also by Dr John Court, for further discussions on adolescent development.*)

In general, it would be reasonable to consult your doctor about early puberty when:

- a girl has shown signs of breast development before the age of nine
- a boy has shown any signs of puberty before the age of ten
- a boy or girl has shown signs of pubic hair development before the age of nine
- anytime you or your child are worried about it

The development of puberty in a boy

Peter was seeing me for quite another reason, but his mother brought up the question of his puberty. It was affecting his moods, she felt, and she wondered what effect it would have on his diabetes.

'Of course, we're not allowed to see him in the bathroom any more,' Peter's mother said. 'I don't really know whether he's starting to develop, but he's very secretive, and there must be an explanation for his bad moods.'

It turned out that Peter was rather amused by his mother's interest in his development. 'Is that why you're always trying to barge into the bathroom just when I'm going to have a shower?' he said. 'I'm thinking of wiring up the bathroom doorhandle to give you an electric shock if you keep butting in.'

'And to think it was only a little while ago that I was bathing him,' his mother said. 'They grow up so quickly these days. I rather miss my dear little boy.'

Peter didn't allow his mother behind the screen while I was examining him, but he got so interested in his testicle size when we checked them out together that he couldn't resist telling her that they were halfway to being ready for making sperm.

'What an awful thought!' said his mother.

Some aspects of puberty in a boy are quite obvious to everyone – the increase in growth rate, the acne, the emotional outbursts. Some are obvious enough to the boy himself, and of great interest to him. These include the development of pubic hair, his growing penis and frequent erections. Some are only of note to a doctor who may become involved if things need to be checked. These include the increasing levels of hormones in the blood, the maturing bone development and the increasing maturity of sexual development.

Some boys become rather modest when they see signs of puberty; most are proud of it

Most boys are reasonably satisfied with the way they are progressing through puberty, though they may wonder if they are really normal and sufficiently well developed for their age. Perhaps they feel that they are slower than other boys, or not developing as well as they would like. If they do worry about this (and most boys do at some time or another) it could be embarrassing to talk about it, even to their parents. Of course, their parents would usually be the best people to discuss any worries about growth, and some boys are quite open about their pubescent development. Some boys proudly display their first pubic hairs to their mother, and feel quite comfortable in discussing erections and sexual feelings with their father. Other boys retreat into embarrassed silence whenever the subject of puberty arises at home.

Puberty usually starts in the pre-teenage years

One thing is certain: puberty in boys often starts in the pre-teenage years. This is the time that parents can prepare their son for his adolescent development, and help with advice and reassurance if he seems worried about his progress.

What is the sequence of events in puberty?

The development of puberty usually follows an orderly pattern and is in the same sequence for boys. But the timing of each event, and the rate that development occurs, can vary a lot between one boy and another of the same age. Boys often compare themselves with each other, and wonder how they are going. It may help them and their parents to know what is happening, and what to expect, in puberty.

The first thing to happen is that the testes start to enlarge

The first outward sign of puberty is enlargement of the testes. The testes are quite small in a boy before puberty, usually between 2 to 3 millilitres in volume. At this stage they are making only small amounts of the hormone testosterone, and no mature sperm. The testes are usually held rather close to the body in their sac, the scrotum; and there is a well-developed muscle that draws the testes into safety, close to the groin, if the boy is nervous or cold. Sometimes this muscle acts so strongly in retracting the testes that it can make it appear that they may not have descended properly into the scrotal sac. It is important to check this out well before puberty, as the testes need to be well outside the abdominal wall, and kept at a slightly cooler temperature than the rest of the body, if they are to develop properly.

When puberty starts, the testes begin to enlarge, and when they are about 4 millilitres in volume we usually consider that puberty has really got under way. At the same time, the scrotal sac that contains the testes also starts to develop and allows the growing testes to hang lower between the legs. Some boys refer to their testicles 'dropping'. It doesn't happen as suddenly as this sounds, and the muscle that draws up the testes towards the groin still works well in protecting them when the boy is cold or nervous.

Pubic hair starts to appear

At about the same time, but often some months or even a year later (occasionally even before the testes have started to enlarge), the boy starts to develop pubic hair just above his penis. This hair growth is rather sparse at first, with just a few hairs that tend to be fairly straight. Gradually, hair growth increases and extends over the pubic region. It is not until a late stage of puberty that they extend downwards and backwards between the legs and, later, in a line upwards towards the navel.

The penis starts to grow later

The penis starts to grow a little later, and not until the testes are further developed. Growth of the penis isn't always obvious at first, and the boy may be rather worried that this isn't happening at the same rate as he would like. At a later stage of puberty his penis will enlarge, first becoming longer and then broader.

It isn't possible to predict how large a boy's penis will become, and there is a wide variation in what is normal. It used to be said (as a consolation for those teenagers who thought they were underdeveloped) that when the mature penis is erect, there is very little difference between one man and another. This isn't true, and it is a pity that many boys set so much store on the size of their penis. At all events, in the pre-teenage years there is so much variation between one boy and another, due to varying stages of puberty, that most of their worries are unfounded. For those boys who are really anxious, there are standard growth charts of the developing penis available, and a paediatrician can use these to reassure a boy that he really is normal.

Erections become more frequent

As the testes produce more of the male hormone testosterone, and the penis develops, the boy will have more erections. Of course, as every parent knows, boys have occasional erections from infancy, but they become much more frequent at puberty. Often erections happen at inconvenient times, such as when a boy is changing for sport, or on the beach. They can happen even when the boy isn't sexually aroused (but he is probably aroused quite a lot of the time at this age). It is as if his penis has a mind of its own. At this stage it is usual for boys to masturbate more often, and this is quite normal.

Some breast enlargement is common in early puberty

At about this time, many boys (probably 40%) develop some swelling of the breast just beneath their nipple. This can happen on just one side at first, and can be quite tender to touch (especially in the physical knocks of football or play-fights). Most boys know this is normal, which it is. However, some boys still worry that they may have got cancer. They feel they would be laughed at if they asked anyone, including their parents, for advice.

Sometimes their breast swelling extends well beyond the nipple area, and this can be very embarrassing for some boys. They may even wonder if they are normal. This happens quite often in boys who are overweight, adding to their misery about their body shape.

This breast development often lasts up to eighteen months or so. It has nearly always disappeared by then, but very occasionally persists. If this happens, and the boy is sensitive about it, it can be quite readily corrected by a plastic surgeon. Parents will guess he is worried if he refuses to go swimming, or wears sweaters in hot weather, or refuses to take his T-shirt off in public.

The boy has his first ejaculation

While all this is happening, other changes are taking place unnoticed inside the boy's body. There are glands beneath the bladder and connected to the tube leading from the bladder to the penis (the urethra). These are the prostate gland and the seminal vesicles and they are small and undeveloped before puberty. They have the function of making semen, the fluid that holds the sperm made in the testes, and then storing this semen and sperm.

When the boy's testes reach a certain size and are producing large amounts of testosterone, the prostate and seminal vesicles will also have enlarged and be capable of storing sperm from the testes and making semen. At this stage the boy starts to ejaculate when he masturbates or sometimes during sleep (wet dreams). Many boys find this rather embarrassing and don't like to talk about it (except amongst themselves perhaps), and unlike a girl having her first period, most mothers may not know when this is happening. The average age when boys are capable of releasing sperm is thirteen, so many pre-teenagers will have had their first ejaculation by then.

When puberty is well advanced, growth rate reaches its peak

Growth in height occurs at a relatively late stage of puberty in boys, and for late developers, this can be a real worry for them.

(See page 23 for a further discussion of growth rates in puberty.)

Then there's acne to worry about

Acne usually starts when adolescence is well under way, and is much more a concern for teenagers than for the pre-teenager. It is due to the increasing levels of the male sex hormones, especially testosterone, which have an effect on the oily glands in the skin, called the sebaceous glands. Teenagers should not have to suffer the worst effects of acne, as there are good treatments for it, provided they persist in using the treatment (which can be asking rather a lot of some teenagers).

(See You and your teenager *for a further discussion on acne.*)

There is further development ahead

Later events of adolescence seldom occur in pre-teenage boys, except in the very early developers. They include the development of body hair, first in the armpit, and later on the face. On the face it first appears on the upper lip, in the moustache area. Later, the hair develops on other parts of the body, such as the chest and legs. There is great variation in the amount of body hair that men have; despite what hairy men might say, it is not a measure of virility.

At about this time the boy's voice starts to break as his voice box (the larynx) enlarges and matures. His chest broadens and his muscle development and strength reaches its peak. This is a late stage of adolescence and usually occurs when the boy is well into the late teens.

The development of puberty in a girl

'*I'm having a lot of trouble talking to Amy about puberty*' her mother told me. '*She has obviously started to develop, and I want to talk to her about hygiene and what to expect about her body changes, but she just clams up.*'

Amy looked daggers at her mother and said that she knew all about periods and stuff, thank you. 'They tell us about it at school.'

'Mum's suddenly got this thing about sex. I just don't want to talk about it,' Amy told me.

I suggested to Amy's mother that Amy would probably decide to talk about it in her own time, and even if she wasn't very enthusiastic about a talk on hygiene, she would most likely listen to some advice and ask for more when the time came.

'Well, she may seem pretty sophisticated and know-all,' said her mother, who I thought was probably a bit hurt that Amy didn't want her advice, and was getting fed up with her moods.

'You don't really know much, and if you won't talk about it to me, you better do some reading,' she said, turning to her twelve-year old daughter.

'Yeah, Mum,' said Amy.

Even though many children do get information at school about adolescent development, many have started puberty well before then. Some don't really absorb much from class instruction, or they get misinformation from friends. It's usually best if parents start talking about puberty quite early. Then it becomes easy to enlarge on the information and answer questions from time to time without making a big thing of it.

Actually Amy's mother was probably right, and there was plenty to talk about when Amy was ready to listen and discuss it. It is always helpful to know what is happening to one's body, and puberty can be pretty confusing for a pre-teenager.

Puberty in a girl starts before there are any outward signs

The first thing that happens at the start of puberty is enlargement of the ovaries as a result of stimulation from hormones from the pituitary gland. The ovaries are quite small in childhood before puberty, and produce only very small amounts of the hormone oestrogen.

When the ovaries start to develop, and increase in size, they produce oestrogen in the small gland-like structures within the ovaries called follicles. The girl will, of course, be unaware of these changes within her body, and the only way that we could know that puberty was under way at this stage would be by measuring the amount of hormones in the blood, or by getting a picture of the ovaries with an ultrasound examination. The ultrasound gives a picture of what is going on inside the abdomen and pelvis, but this is a test that would only be done if there seemed to be a problem that needed investigation.

The oestrogen from the developing ovaries leads to most of the changes that follow. The first thing that a girl will notice, and that will signal that puberty has started, is the development of her breasts. At first there is just a swelling beneath the nipple area. Often this is mainly on one side, and may be quite tender to touch. The other side soon catches up, although unequal development between the two sides is not uncommon and, if it is slight, it is of no consequence. Sometimes a girl may be uncertain if this is normal or not, and it is easy to reassure her if she tells her mother about it. It is perfectly reasonable to ask your family doctor to check it out if there seems to be anything unusual about the early breast development. Sometimes girls hear so much about breast cancer that they worry if they have unequal breast development.

Soon the breasts enlarge further and development extends outwards beyond the nipple area. The swelling under the nipples often continues as a prominent part of the breast, and this is normal. It is not until the breasts become mature as an adult that this prominence beneath the nipple becomes incorporated into the general contour of the breast.

At this stage many pre-teenagers become quite self-conscious and modest. No-one is allowed to see them undressed. Her brother, who only a few years earlier was sharing a bath with her, is banned from her bedroom with shrieks of anguish. Even her mother may not be allowed to know about this development. This is quite usual, but it is more difficult for the girl if she is worried that her breast development is not quite normal, and she feels that she can't talk about it with anyone. Fortunately, she will need to discuss the question of a bra with her mother, and this will give them both a chance to discuss any worries about it.

Pubic hair

About the same time that her breasts are starting to develop, sometimes a little earlier or a little later, pubic hair will start to appear. Although oestrogen does have some control over hair development, pubic hair is mainly under the control of a different hormone. This part of puberty is due to a hormone released from the adrenal glands, which are found just above the kidneys. The adrenal glands, like the ovaries, are also under the control of the pituitary gland; and they usually receive the signals that puberty is due to start from the pituitary gland at about the same time as the ovaries.

The first hairs appear along the labia, which are the lips of the vagina. This is followed by development of hair in the pubic area, which is more obvious to the girl. This hair gradually extends and thickens as puberty proceeds.

The internal sexual development

The ovaries continue to mature, and follicles develop, throughout the pubescent period. This eventually leads to the release of increasing amounts of oestrogen and other hormones that govern the cycles of ovulation and menstruation which will occur when she is a mature woman. The developing follicles within the enlarging ovaries will, in time, become capable of releasing ova. The ovaries of the young girl contain thousands of immature ova, but only a small proportion of these will ever become mature and capable of becoming fertilised.

With the release of oestrogen, the other internal sex organs will also be developing. The vagina is enlarging and is producing mucus. This has a different chemical composition to the mucus produced by the immature vagina, and helps to protect the internal sex organs from infection. There may be quite a lot of mucus, and this may worry the pre-teenage girl. It may seem like a discharge, but it is quite healthy and normal.

The uterus (the womb) is also developing in size and changing in form to prepare it for its eventual role in pregnancy. As this is happening, the lining of the uterus thickens and develops a rich blood supply which would be needed to support a pregnancy. In due course this lining will be shed regularly each month, during the girl's menstrual cycle.

The growth spurt

Girls accelerate their growth rate early in puberty, unlike boys.
(See page 23 for a further discussion on growth rates in puberty.)

Body weight

Another effect of increasing oestrogen levels in the blood is an increase in body weight, partly through the development of body fat. Girls tend to put on weight in early puberty and this is natural, and indeed desirable, for normal development, however much it might annoy the girl as she looks in dismay at herself in the mirror. The development of fat beneath the skin occurs particularly in the breast area, the buttocks, the upper thigh and the lower abdomen. This is where nature intended it to be, but that doesn't always mean that the girl is pleased with the arrangement of nature.

Body shape

The general shape of the girl's body changes throughout puberty, particularly in the later stages. This happens as the bones mature, increasing the size of the pelvis. The bones of the pelvis guard the uterus and bladder with a protective circle of bone around the lower abdomen.

Sometimes girls don't like their broad hips. It is normal, of course, and a sign of becoming a mature woman.

Body hair

Later in puberty, hair develops on other parts of the body; particularly under the armpits, and on the arms and the legs. Sometimes this seems to the girl to be excessive, though it is usually quite normal. If a girl is worried about this, it is reasonable to discuss it with your doctor, as sometimes it can be due to a hormonal imbalance.

Other changes in puberty

Other changes that often occur in puberty include increased oiliness of the skin, which sometimes leads to acne, and the physical changes that will eventually lead to full adult maturity. These occur usually well after the pre-teenage period.

(See You and your teenager *for further discussions on physical changes in the teenage years.)*

The first menstrual period

The first menstrual period occurs towards the end of puberty when most of the rapid growth is over, and many of the early changes of puberty are well under way. This event is called the menarche, and occurs usually two to four years after the breasts have first started to develop.

The first menstrual periods usually occur before the ovaries have started to release ova. Some girls may ovulate with their first period, or soon after. Others may not ovulate for a year or so after their first period.

Periods are often erratic at first and there may be quite a long gap before the next period — even up to six to twelve months. This is usually quite normal.

The average age for girls in Australia to have their first period is just before their thirteenth birthday. This means that 50% of girls will have started to have periods while they are still pre-teenagers.

Growth during puberty: shooting up or slowing down?

'*I am really worried about Jason,*' *his mother said.* '*He seems to have stopped growing.*'

'*I have not, Mum,*' *said her twelve-year-old son. He did not really want to come to see a doctor much, and he had some misgivings about what a physical examination for 'growth and development' might entail.*

'*You haven't grown at all. You are wearing the same jeans I bought you six months ago. And look how all the boys in your class are shooting up and leaving you behind.*'

'*Well, first of all,*' *said Jason,* '*all my friends aren't shooting up like you say; just Adam and maybe Mark. Then second, I'm not the shortest boy in my year, and I'm not being left behind. And third, I like my jeans. That's why I wear them. But I need new shoes.*'

The problem of slow growth in the pre-teenage and early teenage years is mainly one for boys. Girls enter puberty earlier than boys and their rapid growth period is, unlike boys, quite early in puberty. In fact, it is not uncommon to find many girls are actually a bit taller than boys of the same age at this time. This can be a bit annoying for the boys, and the girls are likely to think the boys are very immature (which they probably are). Fortunately for the boys, they tend to catch up quite soon in height, but it will be some years before the girls think boys are as mature as they are themselves.

The fastest rate of growth during childhood is in the first year of life, and from then on growth rate steadily slows down. This slowing down of growth continues into the pre-teenage years, and most boys grow at their slowest rate between the ages of nine till eleven years. In that period the average increase in height in a year is 5 centimetres, some boys grow as little as

4 centimetres, although some will grow as much as 6½ centimetres. From the age of twelve, most boys start to grow more rapidly, on average growing 7 centimetres that year and over 9 centimetres when they are thirteen. But the range of growth rates in perfectly normal boys is quite wide. A late-developing twelve-year-old may still only grow 4 centimetres that year, while another boy who is well into puberty might grow as much as 10 centimetres.

Most children and teenagers still like to know their height in feet and inches, even though they may have a very hazy idea of how long a foot or an inch really is. It is probably due to the achievement of reaching 5 feet, which about 50% of boys do when they are in their twelfth year, and the challenge of reaching 6 feet, which many boys aspire to, but only about 15% actually achieve.

If we say that 94% of children in our society fall within a 'normal' range in height (which isn't quite fair, as many normal children fall outside that range, including the 3% who will be shorter), it may help to decide whether a child who seems to be short, or growing too slowly, is really normal or perhaps should be checked over by a doctor. It may also help to decide whether a very tall girl falls outside a normal range and whether any concern about her becoming too tall as an adult should be considered.

The following table sets out heights of boys and girls in our society. The table gives average heights and also a range of heights that are found in children in their pre-teenage years. At the lower end of the range, although 97% of children will be taller, there will still be 3% who are shorter. At the upper end of the range, 97% of children will be shorter, but there will still be 3% who are taller.

Average and ranges of height in boys

Heights are shown in centimetres (cm). Brackets show height in feet and inches.

Age	Average	Lower end of range for most boys	Upper end of range for most boys
9	135 cm (4ft 5)	124 cm (4ft 1)	145 cm (4ft 9)
10	140 cm (4ft 7)	128 cm (4ft 2½)	152 cm (5ft)
11	146 cm (4ft 9½)	133 cm (4ft 4½)	160 cm (5ft 3)
12	156 cm (5ft 1½)	138 cm (4ft 6½)	168 cm (5ft 6)

Average and ranges of height in girls

Age	Average	Lower end of range for most girls	Upper end of range for most girls
9	135 cm (4ft 5)	122 cm (4ft 0)	147 cm (4ft 10)
10	142 cm (4ft 8)	128 cm (4ft 2½)	154 cm (5ft 1)
11	149 cm (4ft 11)	135 cm (4ft 5)	161 cm (5ft 3½)
12	155 cm (5ft 1)	142 cm (4ft 8)	167 cm (5ft 6)

These figures for height may give a guide as to whether your child is very unusual, or really within a normal range. The fact that most of their friends are taller doesn't mean a child is abnormal. If a child's mother or father is short, then it isn't surprising that their children are more likely to be short. On the other hand, if a child is short but parents are relatively tall, there may be something that is interfering with the expected growth rate which needs sorting out.

Can anything be done about very short children?

Most parents want their children to grow to their natural potential. In our society most children, particularly boys, feel it is better to be tall, and the taller the better. No-one can make a child grow taller than nature intended safely, but we can certainly work out if something is preventing a child from growing to their natural potential. It is better to resolve this during the pre-teens rather than leaving it until adolescence, when it may be too late to make much change in the final adult height.

If either a parent or a pre-teenager is worried about growth, they should discuss it with their doctor, even if the pre-teen's height appears to fall within the normal range shown in the table above. It becomes more important if the height falls outside the normal range, particularly if this doesn't seem to be in keeping with the rest of the family.

The family doctor will probably refer the pre-teenager to a specialist if he thinks there may be a problem. Certain tests may help to sort it out. Some of these tests will be aimed to rule out things that can interfere with growth (like diseases that prevent proper absorption of nutrients from the digestive system) and some may check out the hormones that control growth. Usually it is helpful to check how the bones are maturing by taking an X-ray of the wrist and hand. This will tell if the pre-teen is growing slowly because of late development (which is usually not due to any serious cause), and may help to make an estimate of final adult height.

If a cause can be found for slow growth and short stature, it may be that reassurance and an estimate of what to expect as adult height will be all that is needed. On the other hand, most disease and hormonal causes of short stature can be treated. Of course, if poor growth is due to deficiency of hormones in the body, these can be replaced through tablets or injections, depending on which hormones are lacking.

Sometimes, as a very short boy approaches adolescence and some hurrying up of growth seems important, it is possible to give a short course of hormonal treatment to get growth started. This may have psychological benefit, but it will be important to ensure that any treatment that hurries up growth doesn't interfere with the final adult stature.

Can anything be done for very tall girls?

Many mothers who are very tall remember the agonies of embarrassment they felt socially as teenagers, and young adults, through being much taller than everyone else. Some pre-teenage girls already feel the same way. They tend to stoop when they are with their friends, as girls like to be at eye level with each other. They don't always like to be different, especially when adults treat them as being older than they really are, and expect more of them than is reasonable for their age.

If a pre-teenage, very tall girl or her mother is worried about tall stature (especially whether the girl might end up 6 feet or taller as an adult) it is perfectly reasonable to discuss it with their doctor, who may refer the problem to a specialist in childhood growth. It is possible to calculate the expected adult height by taking an X-ray of the wrist and hand to find out how much growth potential there is in the bones. The bones of the wrist and hand can tell us about the maturity of the rest of the skeleton, and help estimate how much future growth to expect.

If it looks as if a pre-teenage girl is heading for an adult stature of greater than 5 feet 11, and both the pre-teenager and her family are sure that this would be a disadvantage socially, it is reasonable and safe to give hormonal treatment to limit the final adult height. This treatment should not be started before puberty is under way with early breast development, but it also shouldn't be left too late. It probably won't have much effect once the girl has started her menstrual period.

What about Jason? When I measured him and checked him out, I found that he was certainly short, but well inside the normal range. As his father was rather short there didn't seem much mystery about his height, and he knew who to blame (his father for giving him short-stature genes, and his mother for worrying about him). He had only just started puberty, so there was plenty of growth ahead of him. We checked his bone maturity with an X-ray, and this reassured both him and his mother about how tall he would probably reach as an adult: just a bit taller than his father. For Jason, that was the best part of the consultation.

After all that, Jason said he'd like to come back in six months just to check that my calculations about his expected growth were correct and to make sure that he was on target for normal growth. 'By the way,' I told his mother, 'one of the earliest signs of growth at puberty is when the feet are getting bigger.'

'In that case,' Jason's mother said to him, 'perhaps we will get you some new shoes after all.'

Early emotional changes at puberty

Most pre-teenagers are only just starting puberty, and many of the emotional upheavals so common in adolescence will not be affecting them for some time. But many pre-teenagers, particularly those who started puberty early, do have some of the confusing emotions and feelings that happen at this stage.

The sex hormones not only cause the physical and sexual development of puberty, but also affect how people behave and feel. Parents may notice changes in mood and emotions before the physical changes of puberty become evident. The hormones of puberty start to rise well before there are any obvious changes so that sometimes emotional changes occur before there has been much physical change.

Of course, sometimes pre-teenagers hide the early physical signs of puberty (such as pubic hair development or early breast changes) from their parents, but they can hardly hide the emotional swings.

Changes in emotions and behaviour as puberty approaches will be quite obvious in some pre-teenagers, while others will experience very little, if any, change. It partly depends on the stage of pubescent development, partly on the child's own temperament and personality, and partly on how the family responds to the mood changes and behaviour difficulties. And, of course, friends and peer groups are now starting to exert a strong influence on social behaviour.

What can parents expect as puberty starts?

MOOD SWINGS

Most children get into bad moods at times. There is usually a reason for them, even though their parents may not know what it is. There may have been a fight with a sibling or a friend at school, or perhaps someone has hurt their feelings. At puberty these mood swings tend to become more frequent and more intense, and sometimes the cause for them seems less obvious than usual. Pre-teens are much more likely to become upset by things someone has said about them (or what they imagine they have said), or frustrated by little things that have gone wrong.

Quite often there doesn't seem any reason for the bad moods. When parents ask what the matter is the pre-teenager says 'Nothing' or 'I don't know' and then bursts into tears and rushes off to their room. There are slammed doors and shouts of 'Leave me alone'. This is very frustrating to parents who are trying to help their pre-teenager and cheer them up. Usually, if you do leave them alone for a little while to cool off, the problem (whatever it was) is forgotten. They might cheer up if someone else goes in after a little while, when they have cooled off, and talks to them. They might want to tell someone, maybe an elder sister, what was upsetting them. Perhaps all they needed was for someone to distract them with a joke or a game.

Sometimes when pre-teenagers are in a bad mood they don't seem to really want to get out of it, and resist all efforts to be cheered up. It's almost as if they are enjoying their bad moods. This is a very good reason to make sure there is somewhere they can go by themselves for a while, and not inflict their bad mood on everyone else. Perhaps they could go outside and do something energetic. Most likely they will just go and sulk in their room until they get bored by being miserable, and jealous that everyone else seems to be having a good time. Then they might be ready for someone to go and get them to rejoin the family.

Of course, if the bad moods go on and on, or are becoming very frequent, it could mean that something is really troubling them, and they may need help to sort it out.

BAD TEMPERS

Even easy-going children seem to get outbursts of bad temper when they go into puberty. Things seem to annoy them more, and they might develop a rather short fuse. This is much more true for children who are naturally quarrelsome, or have the kind of temperament that makes them easily put out if something goes wrong. It doesn't mean that the family has to put up with the bad behaviour, but it does help if parents understand that the hormones of puberty are part of the reason why tempers can flare up so easily.

Parents still have to curb bad behaviour and try to help their pre-teenager control their feelings and the way they express them. But they may need 'time out to cool off' more often.

SECRETIVE

Children who have always shared their thoughts and worries with their parents may start to be rather secretive, when they reach puberty, about what they are thinking or what is upsetting them. Sometimes it is because they are confused about their worries and do not know how to express them. Sometimes they feel ashamed or embarrassed about some of the things that happen to them (such as being teased), or that they feel (such as their sexual feelings). Sometimes they may not want to worry their parents about a topic they feel is private or very personal.

This is the age of secret diaries of girls, of secret (and usually rather grubby) jokes of boys, of private friendship groups and shared naughtiness. Sometimes it's just as well parents don't know all the things that their pre-teenagers get up to or think about.

CHALLENGING AND ARGUING
Puberty is a time for children to start reviewing their social relationship with peers and their reliance on their parents. As they proceed through adolescence they will begin to challenge the views and opinions of their parents. They may argue when previously they were prepared to do what they were told, even if they didn't like it. The pre-teenager may be more impressed by the views of other adults or other pre-teenagers. All this is basically a good thing and a necessary part of growing up, but even so it can be very frustrating to parents, who feel that they really do know what is best for their child. And all the arguing can be very trying.

It is the first stage in the very important task of standing on their own two feet in adult life, and becoming less dependent on their parents.

EXPERIMENTING
Pre-teenagers often look for new experiences. They want to find things out for themselves. What is it like to smoke a cigarette? How does it feel to do something naughty? It is sometimes exciting to explore sexual feelings, and share them with someone else. What does alcohol taste like? Let's light a fire in the rubbish bin and see what happens.

Some people may think this sort of behaviour is silly and risk-taking (and it may be so) but often it is just a case of pre-teens finding things out for themselves, and sometimes not thinking of consequences.

FRIENDSHIPS

Pre-teenagers, particularly girls, are starting to form strong friendship groups. These may be very close and intense. Sometimes they may be quite exclusive, and not allow any other girls to be part of the group. It is the age of very best friends, of soul mates. Unfortunately, it is also the age of changing friendships, of feeling let down or excluded. It is a time when girls may think others are saying things about them, as well they might.

Boys also may form friendship groups, but the groups tend to be looser and less exclusive. For boys it may be the start of involvement in gangs; although they may get up to mischief together, they are usually fairly harmless at this age. It is usual for the sexes to keep apart in their groups, although boy—girl friendships can be quite close and affectionate. As adolescence progresses, peer relationships and influence will become more important and will increasingly dominate the social life of the adolescent.

Sexual orientation: 'Could I be gay'?

A generation or so ago, parents didn't worry much whether their child might be homosexual. On the whole, it didn't occur to parents that this was a possibility. Children and teenagers didn't get too worried about it, either. Schoolgirl 'crushes' on another girl, especially an older girl or a female teacher or sports-mistress, were thought to be absolutely natural (and so they were), something they would grow out of (which they did) and part of growing up (which it was).

Similar thoughts amongst boys were mostly denied by mothers, who knew from their own experience how pre-teenage girls felt, but not how boys felt. Fathers, on the whole, didn't think it was manly to talk about feelings, sexual or otherwise, with their sons. If they did talk about sex at all with their pre-teenage son, it would be about the wonderful times they would have with girls that they would meet one day when they were 'men'.

So, boys had to work out their feelings and behaviour for themselves. What they usually felt was sexual excitement with their own body and genital development. Boys handle their penis many times every day when they pass urine. They often see each other at school when they change for sport, and in toilets where boys stand in line to empty their bladder. They may look and compare and discuss. Erections are particularly interesting, and occur from early childhood, but happen more frequently as boys enter puberty. Naturally, if a boy is interested in his own and other boys' genital development, and has so many opportunities to examine what's going on, it would lead to mutual discussions and, perhaps, sexual encounters and explorations.

Boys usually thought this was pretty harmless and natural. The only problem was that they knew that adults heavily disapproved of any boy having sexual thoughts or encounters, and mothers usually warned their sons it was 'dirty' and something to be ashamed about. So the encounters, if they occurred, were secret and exciting because they were forbidden. Although boys had been taught it was morally wrong to touch their own or other boys' genitals, they seldom thought of it as homosexual behaviour. It was just part of being a boy growing up. Homosexuals were men, and if they were talked about much at all, they were regarded as abnormal men whose behaviour was 'queer'. They were often subjected to shame and abuse because of sexual behaviour, which was all right when they were boys, but which they should have grown out of after adolescence.

People now have very different attitudes towards homosexual behaviour. The term 'gay' has replaced some of the really derogatory words that used to be used. The community now largely accepts the fact that gay men are no different from other men, except in their sexual orientation. The prevalence of AIDS has probably made the problem of community acceptance of homosexual behaviour more difficult, and the subject much more talked about, but it has also helped people to feel much more compassionate towards gay men than they ever did before.

Strangely enough, as these community attitudes to gay men have changed towards understanding and acceptance, the attitudes of boys seem to have changed in the opposite direction. What used to be thought of as rather harmless sexual behaviour — such as interest in each other's genital development, and minor sexual encounters between boys (including mutual masturbation) — is now the subject of teasing and derision. In most schools, boys are quite outspoken about their attitude towards any boy who might be gay or who might show interest in male sexuality. I have known boys who have had to change schools because of the bullying and teasing they received about their perceived sexual preference. Perhaps some of the most outspoken boys are unsure themselves about their own sexual orientation. Girls tend to be much more tolerant towards gay boys, and often quite supportive.

These days it can be very difficult for a boy who is unsure of his sexuality. It has been estimated that at least 10% of boys in their early puberty (which is often when they are in their pre-teens or early teens) have homosexual thoughts and experience confusion about whether this may mean that they are gay. They can hardly discuss this with their friends, who would probably be very unhelpful because it wouldn't do to be associated with a boy who is gay, in case everyone assumed you were gay yourself. They can hardly discuss this with their parents, who would either be horrified or might dismiss it as 'something you will grow out of, so don't worry'. It would take a lot of courage to discuss the subject with anyone at all.

However, there are many people, including counsellors and paediatricians and psychologists, who could be very helpful to boys who are troubled about their sexual orientation. They may be able to reassure a pre-teen boy that thoughts about people of the same sex are common and natural. Most young men can be excited sexually about all kinds of sexual activity, including that with someone of the same sex. A pre-teenage boy's feelings are very private; but they are not shameful, and not necessarily indicative of sexual orientation.

Of course, some boys know that they are gay, even as a pre-teenager, although they may be very confused about it. For them it can be difficult and lonely during the teenage years unless there is someone that they can talk to about it and who can help them to work things out comfortably for themselves.

How can parents tell if their pre-teen is worried by their sexual orientation?

Parents will know how difficult it can be for a child to discuss anything so emotive as sexuality with any adult, especially parents. But they may drop hints. Things that may alert parents include:

- asking a lot of questions about gay people
- being teased at school about being gay
- showing an interest in gay magazines
- having been sexually abused
- None of these things mean that a child is at great risk of being gay, but they can mean that he is worried about it.

What can parents do? Should they just ignore the subject?

Parents who think that their child's sexual feelings or behaviour may be worrying them should consider getting help for their pre-teen. Although most boys will work things out perfectly well in time, some will be very troubled, particularly as they will have to live in a teenage world of intolerance towards anyone who seems different, particularly in sexual preference. It is likely that their child will be very embarrassed about the whole matter, so it would take some very tactful discussions before involving anyone else. Several times I have had a pre-teen or a teenager brought along thinking the consultation was for some physical complaint, only to find the real reason was a concern about their sexuality. Sometimes the child has been relieved to have the chance to talk about it, but usually it has been a shock and an embarrassment unless their parent has discussed it with them first, and explained that it is a common concern of parents and teenagers and not something to be ashamed about.

Getting things in place so they won't go wrong

On being useful around the house: jobs and chores

Kate's mother was in despair with her.

She wouldn't help with the washing up. 'Why should I? Dale never does, either.'

She wouldn't help with the vacuuming. 'It's boring.'

She wouldn't put out the rubbish bin for collection. 'That's Mary's job.'

Her room was a mess. 'I like it that way, and it's none of your business.'

She hardly ever fed the dog, even though they had agreed it was her responsibility. 'I do sometimes.'

She never helps with the ironing. 'You're joking. As if I would.'

It wasn't as if she didn't have time: she spent hours on the phone and watching TV. And it wasn't as if her mother couldn't have done with the help after coming home from work and getting the dinner ready for the family. 'I have never asked her to do anything around the house when she was younger, but now that I really need her help, she resents my even asking.'

Kate had just entered her teenage years, and her mother wondered why she hated helping around the house. Quite apart from the fact that Kate's mother would have liked help, she felt it would be good training for Kate to learn to help others.

Kate's mother wondered where she had gone wrong, because she knew that many teenagers do take responsibility for household chores without minding too much. But they need to start long before the teenage years.

Young children like to be useful

Young children usually love to help and do things around the house with their parents. They start being interested in this when they are toddlers. At that age they like being with their parents and trying to copy what they are doing. It may be a game, but they enjoy helping and love to be praised when they are trying to help. However, at that age they are probably more in the way than helping. When they are a little older, children can be given jobs around the house or garden that they can manage, and then they really can be useful. After all, families learn to help each other, and that way children earn the respect of other members through being part of the family and sharing the family chores.

But there seems to be only a short time in their childhood when they willingly help their parents. It's part of belonging to the family, of enjoying being praised by their parents and of being valued as members of the family. If parents don't give them responsible jobs when they are young children, they may not grow up feeling any need to contribute to the family. If parents leave it too late to ask for help around the house, their teenager might resent doing anything at all. They might only do their chores when they are reminded, nagged and yelled at. Parents might resort to bribery by paying teenagers to do something that they would happily have done when they were younger, and would have continued to do.

Start early in childhood, well before the teenage years

Get in well before they hit their teens. It's good for them to be helpful and it's good training for their future role in society. It's good for them to feel that they are contributing to the family, and good for you as a parent to have some of the work around the house shared by the family. And when they are as big and strong as teenagers, they can be really useful.

Discuss with your pre-teen what jobs they feel they could do. Make sure that there is a time for them to do the jobs and then put it into a regular routine so they get into a habit, and don't forget. Give them plenty of praise and thanks, but don't pay them for helping.

Don't link chores with pocket money

Ideally, jobs should be quite separate from pocket money or allowances. Otherwise your pre-teen isn't really helping you as part of belonging to the family. It could lead to bargaining and demanding money before they do something that they have undertaken to do. They might argue that the money isn't worth it, and that they could get a better paying job somewhere else. (That's fine, but their job at home doesn't get done, and you don't get help.)

Make sure that your pre-teenager knows that you rely on them and appreciate their help.

Kate was prepared to admit that her mother had a lot of work to do for the family and could do with some help, even though she told her mother that it was her own fault that she was so overworked. Kate suggested a chore she could do that didn't interfere with her busy social life. It wasn't much, but it was something. Kate's family then had a discussion over dinner (Kate had made a cake to help achieve harmony and good will), and the rest of the family were also given some tasks. Her eleven-year-old brother felt quite proud that he had been invited to join in the family discussion, and actually volunteered which jobs he thought he could do.

Rules and routine: 'How boring'

Young children tend to rely on their parents to tell them when to do things. They expect to be told when to go to bed, brush their hair, get their school books ready, pack their lunch and feed the guinea pig. Young children know that they have to be reminded, and they usually don't mind too much when their parents tell them to do these things

On the other hand, teenagers hate to be told these things, even though they will probably forget to do them quite often, or do them late. Teenagers often waste a lot of time doing nothing (or they seem to be doing nothing — who knows?) and this is especially annoying for parents when they should be getting things done. If teenagers don't have a regular routine in their life, they may spend a lot of their time wondering what to do. They find excuses for putting off doing things they don't want to do; and then they can't work out when to do homework or where to find their clean clothes. They don't have time to do household chores or personal things like taking their asthma medication and making their bed. When they are told to do something, they get cross and accuse their mother of nagging. (Fathers don't nag — they just go ballistic; but the effect may be the same.)

Many young people say they really hate rules for behaviour and having to stick to a regular routine. Actually they are the very things that most teenagers need to help them get through the adolescent process of becoming independent, so they do not need to rely on their family and school as much. But for family rules and routine to be acceptable and helpful, they need to be in place before they become teens. If teenagers haven't got used to some rules and didn't get into a routine when they were pre-teens, they might resent them imposed as they grow older. And the rules will be much more difficult to enforce.

Rules and routine often go together. It makes life easier, rather than harder, for everyone, especially teenagers, if there are firm rules about behaviour and routine in the family. It provides a framework for daily living, so that children can get the boring things of life done without too much hassle and argument. Most parents know this, but sometimes well-meaning people say that teenagers don't need rules because it only gives them something to rebel against, and provides an excuse for fights at home.

Nothing could be further from the truth. Rules and routine provide the firm ground from which teenagers can set off to discover new experiences and to which they can return for safety and recuperation when things get difficult. Another thing: if there aren't any rules, how can a teenager try testing them? And then how will they get to know what is expected of them? Or how will they learn self-discipline and self-control?

Rules and routine need to be firmly in place in their pre-teens

The pre-teenage years give parents a window in time to get themselves and their children ready for the rebellious period ahead. Now is the time to prepare them to take more responsibility in their lives through planning a routine that fits in with the family, and allows them to do all the things they want and need to do. When this is done, and accepted by the pre-teen, parents can relax and look forward to the teenage years ahead.

Routine: all families are different

Some families are pretty disorganised. Other families have very strict rules and routines. It all depends on what parents like best for their family, how easy it is for them to be organised themselves, and the culture in which they have grown up. Some parents say they are so busy themselves that they just don't have time to impose a routine on their children: they have to get on with their lives themselves. Other parents say that because they are so busy, they can only cope if the family fits into a routine with everyone knowing exactly what is expected of them. Some parents feel that children have to work things out for themselves and learn from their own actions. If they don't get their homework done, or if they lose their sports clothes, or if they are late for school or if their room's a mess, too bad. They can learn from taking the consequences, like having detentions, sleeping in an uncomfortable bed or missing sport. Other parents want to protect their children from the worst of these consequences, and hope that their children can learn to look after themselves without getting hurt.

All these views are fine if they suit the family. No-one can tell parents how to bring up their children. But if things aren't working out well, or if parents want to look ahead at what is in store for their children when they become teenagers, they might want to consider how a regular routine in their daily life can help their children go through adolescence.

Here are some of the ways you might make sure your pre-teen gets into a routine.

BEDTIME

It is very easy for pre-teens to start putting off going to bed. Then they will probably be tired in the morning when it's time to get up for school. This becomes a major problem for many pre-teens and teenagers who seem to come alive at night when everyone else is ready for bed. Many studies have suggested that most teenagers are regularly short on sleep, so it's good to agree on a sensible time for bed (at least on school days) and make it a rule.

HOUSEHOLD CHORES

You should have these in place long before your child becomes a teenager, and certainly by their pre-teens, when your children can be really useful. If it's part of a routine, chores don't seem so hard to do. If children have to be reminded all the time, chores tend to become a battleground. Many parents will then give up in disgust, and end up feeding the dog or putting out the rubbish themselves because otherwise it wouldn't get done.

HOMEWORK

Most children realise that homework has to be done. If they don't do it, it is likely that their teacher will want to know why, and with any luck, parents can leave this for the school to sort out. But some children have a lot of difficulty in settling down to study after school or at night. There always seems to be something better to do. They need to relax after all the stress of school. There's something they really want to watch on TV. The phone rings and they have to talk for hours to a friend.

If this threatens to be a problem, get a homework routine in place at the start of secondary school, when it starts to be important. Agree how much study needs to be done each night. The school could help with this. At age twelve, an hour is usually plenty. Go through the week and plan with your pre-teen when this homework is going to be done. Straight after school when they get home and have had a snack? When they get in from playing with friends at a set time? Straight after the evening meal? Maybe it has to be varied according to sports training or youth club or a TV show, but an agreed routine makes it easier for everyone. No need to argue: that's the rule that was agreed on for homework. It will pay dividends during the teenage years.

TELEVISION

The same is true for TV. Some pre-teens spend hours each day watching TV. It becomes a habit, and gets in the way of exercise, family meals, homework, playing with friends and bedtime. If this seems to be happening, set rules. Make sure that you are comfortable about the number of hours a day they spend watching TV. Plan in advance, perhaps when the TV programme guide comes out, and agree to which shows your pre-teen can watch. Maybe you can't be too rigid, but rules are rules, and TV is very addictive and intrusive. That's why it can be helpful to plan and avoid arguments.

HYGIENE

Some pre-teens are very conscious about hygiene and being clean. Some get very sloppy as they enter puberty. In that case, when they become teenagers, personal cleanliness, teeth cleaning and the time spent in the bathroom, can all be an excuse for noisy argument. Get in first with rules when they are pre-teens.

FAMILY MEALS

Make it a rule that everyone sits down to a family meal at night, at least most nights; especially the pre-teen who has so many other distractions. Many of the most successful and satisfactory family routines that regulate peaceful life at home are made around meals.

GETTING READY FOR SCHOOL

Some children are so well organised that they are dressed, lunchbox packed, hair brushed and ready for school in good time every day. Some children are always running late, and need help getting their things together every day. For them, it gets worse in their teens when they are likely to be tired and confused first thing in the morning, and assignments and school books are probably scattered all over the place. It is a lot less stressful for everyone if they can get into a structured routine and try to stick to it.

GOING OUT AND COMING HOME

Parents, of course, insist that they know where their children are after school when they are young. This may become a bit harder when the children are older and more independent. However, it is always essential that pre-teens get into the routine of telling their parents where they are, especially at night, and agree to be home at the specified time. This must be an absolute rule for teenagers, and pre-teens should get into the routine of keeping their parents informed and obeying the rules of coming home on time. At least they should phone if something delays them.

Rules and routines don't need to be too rigid

Although it's important for parents to be firm about rules, and it's essential to enforce rules that are needed for safety, sometimes it is possible to be too rigid. This is likely to cause problems as pre-teens enter puberty and start testing the rules and boundaries of behaviour. It can be confusing if their family rules are different from those of their friends. It's always a good idea to discuss rules with your pre-teenager, and be prepared to review them. They will feel they have contributed to decisions about what they can do and what they shouldn't do.

Belonging

Loretta had never belonged anywhere much. Her parents had separated when she was two, and she didn't remember her father at all. When she was four, his mother developed a mental illness which meant she couldn't look after her properly, and she went from one foster home to another. Later, she had to change schools frequently whenever she moved house. Sometimes her mother was well enough to care for her, but by the age of nine she was so insecure with all the changes of care that she had received, that her mother had real trouble in managing her. Over the years, she had been seen by psychiatrists, psychologists, social workers and school counsellors, all of whom had tried to help her and the people who were responsible for her care. None of them seemed to have helped her much, but they all agreed that what she needed was a stable home.

Now that she was aged twelve, she was street-wise, wagged school, smoked and needed a community worker to supervise her. No-one held out much hope for her as a teenager.

This very unfortunate girl was an exceptional case. But she did point up what may happen to a child who has no real basis for a secure childhood or a stable home to grow up in. This girl's experience may be extreme, but not so unusual considering how many marriages now break down, and how many families seem so unstable. Many parents are aware that their marital difficulties may affect their children but they may not realise how much a child can feel disconnected from their family when the basis of the family is under threat.

Quite clearly what Loretta lacked, and what is needed by so many pre-teens and teenagers, is not so much professional help as a sense of feeling connected to a family and some continuity in care.

Recent research by a group in the USA studied why some teenagers got into trouble and some did not. After all, not all children who have disadvantages in life or who come from broken homes get into trouble. The researchers concluded that those young people who coped well with their lives had inner strengths that they termed *resilience*. Resilience referred to the ability to withstand the many difficulties and dangers of being a teenager in a modern society. Foremost in the things that helped children develop a sense of resilience was the feeling of belonging somewhere. For young children, including pre-teens, belonging to a family is the most important thing. Later, young people get strength from belonging to their school, to their group of friends, to their church perhaps, and to other groups such as scouts or their football or basketball team.

Pre-teenagers sometimes feel excluded from their family

Another boy, just eleven, was brought along because he was caught smoking, and had tried to wag school (but he had got caught: 'Just my luck,' he said). Unlike Loretta, James seemed to be part of a caring family. When his mother brought him to discuss why he was being so difficult, his elder brother and younger sister came along too.

James told me that he always seemed to be the one that was a nuisance to his family. 'I suppose I deserve all I get,' he said. 'But I don't seem to do anything right, even when I try. My brother is better at football, and Dad goes to watch him play all the time at weekends.

My little sister is the goody-goody and can't do anything wrong according to Mum and Dad. They even arrange family outings without telling me anything about it. They'd probably all be much happier if I wasn't there.'

Parents can help their children develop the strengths to withstand the difficulties of the teenage years by keeping their family ties strong, and by ensuring that their pre-teenager feels part of the family. Grandparents can help to keep their grandchildren together with the family, and if there are marital difficulties between parents, the continuity of care provided by grandparents often allows a child to still feel part of their family, even though their parents are breaking away from each other.

Another way for a pre-teen to feel part of their family is to give them some responsibility within the family. It should not just be the unpopular jobs so often given to teenagers, like putting out the rubbish, doing the dishes or vacuuming the living room. It may be they will feel more responsible if they help care for a younger brother or sister, perhaps helping with their homework or playing a game with them before bed (assuming that there's nothing better on TV, in which case your pre-teen may feel resentful).

Pre-teenagers need to feel special to their parents. Whether they are part of a large family, or they have just one sibling, there should be times when they do something with their father or mother just by themselves. After all, it is likely that the younger children get moments alone with their parents, perhaps when they are being bathed or read to in bed. It is all very well to say that you do everything together as a family, and of course that is how families should work, but it can also be very helpful to recognise that each child, including pre-teenagers, needs to feel special to their parents at times. This will reinforce their feeling that they are truly part of their family and are important to it.

James seemed a rather sad boy. It didn't help being the middle child with a very successful older brother and a little sister who charmed everyone. He felt that he was a failure to his parents, and his misbehaviour was probably an expression of this sense of failure. When he got punished it just reinforced his feeling that he was no good and his parents didn't want him.

There were no real problems for James. His parents had been hardly aware of his distress, but as they listened to him pouring out his misery they made plans to involve him more in the family activities and spend more time with him. Even his big brother decided to stop stirring him and started to teach him skate boarding.

Pocket money

Robert was discussing his dissatisfaction with 'the management' who made the rules at home. That meant mostly Mum, but Dad wasn't much better, and his elder sister was no help at all. He had decided that as I had known him for three weeks, I could be an independent arbiter. Someone who was 'independent' meant someone who was basically on his side. His mother went along with this, particularly as she was starting to dread the years ahead when he became a teenager.

'To start with,' said Robert, as he settled back in his chair, 'I get hardly any pocket money compared to my friends, and I have to buy my school lunches out of it'.

'You don't have to buy your lunches at all. I offer to cut you sandwiches every day, and there's always plenty of things you could take to school to eat,' his mother cut in.

'Oh yeah?' said Robert. 'What about the other day when there wasn't any bread in the house, and last week when Trudy pinched all the good stuff to eat. You know I hate ham.'

'Well, you didn't seem to mind buying a pie at school those days, did you?'

'That's not the point,' said Robert, who had pretty good arguing skills. 'And another thing, you always cut out my allowance when I am naughty, which isn't fair.'

'I don't know how else to punish you,' his mother said in her defence. 'Why should we pay you money when you don't do your chores, and you answer back and are unkind and rude to your sister when she tries to make you help around the house?'

Considering his sister was seventeen, and Robert was twelve, he thought that was a joke.

This debate could have gone on and on, and probably did at home from time to time. We decided to focus on the question of pocket money — what was reasonable for him to expect, whether he should have to work for it, and whether it should be at risk as punishment for doing bad things. Did Robert have responsibilities, as well as the right to have pocket money?

All children need to have some money that they can spend how they want to. It isn't just a question of fulfiling their need to have things; it helps them develop responsibility in handling money, in budgeting to make sure it lasts until next week, to save for something they really want, or to buy birthday and Christmas presents for the family. All parents recognise this, but does their pre-teenager use their money in this way, or do they just use it on impulse buying? If so, are they ready to learn about money and the hard facts of economy and financial survival?

Pre-teenagers can learn about budgeting and money

Pre-teenagers are old enough to learn how to use their money wisely, to budget ahead and save if they need something they can't afford just now. If they don't learn at this age it gets much harder in the teenage years, when they are much more influenced by their social peers and have so many temptations to spend money, fostered by the commercial world of fashionable clothes, CDs, fast foods and entertainment (not to say cigarettes and alcohol). Sensible spending and careful budgeting don't always come naturally with adult life. I know many young people starting out on their own in life who regularly find there's nothing much to eat in their refrigerator towards the end of the week before the next pay comes in, because they spent too much money on other things they didn't really need earlier in the week.

Of course it is good for children to make their own decisions and their own mistakes about money. That is the way to learn, and the time to learn is in their pre-teens.

How much pocket money should pre-teenagers get?

This should depend on how much the family can afford, and what parents think is reasonable for their pre-teenager to have. Parents should not be influenced by how much children in other families get. Some parents give their children what seem to be very large sums of money each week; and it often gets spent on sweets, drinks, magazines or comics, CDs and games that the pre-teenager doesn't really need and doesn't really appreciate. Parents would be wise to limit pocket money, even though they could afford to be more generous, because it may not be a good way to learn about money. And most families can't be absolutely sure there will always be plenty of money to spare.

Pre-teenagers can understand that their family has to spend money wisely, and that pocket money has to be related to the family budget. It may seem unfair at times that some of their friends have much more money than they do, but that is a fact of life. It is worth discussing this with your pre-teenager, who will accept the decision you make about how much pocket money you can afford and how much you think is reasonable. The major cause of resentment occurs when the pre-teenager builds up unrealistic expectations about how much pocket money they should get.

Should pocket money be spent on necessities like clothes, school lunches and fares?

This depends on how you are teaching your pre-teenager to value money, and whether you think he or she is ready to budget for necessities. Most pre-teenagers aren't quite ready to cope with having large sums of money that they have to use for buying things they need (and which other parents usually get for their children), although some seem to be. But most can't, and if they make mistakes and spend money unwisely, should they suffer as a consequence, or should parents make up the difference?

Having a set allowance to spend on clothes, entertainment and social arrangements can be a valuable way to learn about money when children are mature enough to plan ahead and show responsibility. It is certainly worthwhile later in their teens. If you do decide to give your pre-teenager some responsibility in spending money by allocating some of it to paying for things like fares, clothes and school lunches, you should spend time each week helping them think about their budget, and planning their spending. There should always be some money left over for them to spend on whatever they want, however unwise you may think their decision to be.

Should pocket money be given as payment for doing jobs around the house?

My own view is no. Pre-teenagers should see household chores and jobs around the house as their contribution to helping the family, part of belonging to their home. Everyone has to do things for the family, whether it is by earning money to support the family, or cooking the meals, or cleaning the house, or caring for the family pet. Every contribution by each member of the family has value, but not just in the currency of money.

*(See page 46 for a discussion of the importance
of belonging to a family.)*

Every family, of course, has their own views about this, and what works for one family may not be right for another. Perhaps special jobs, such as particularly unpleasant ones, or ones that would otherwise need a tradesman called in, could be rewarded in some way, including with money. This could be fair and act as an encouragement. But it should not become a routine, or come to be expected. Otherwise, as a teenager you may find that they put a monetary value on everything they do and put little value on helping the family for its own sake.

It is easier all round if pocket money is seen as quite independent of household jobs, except in the sense that the right of receiving pocket money goes along with the responsibility of helping the family.

Should pocket money be withheld as a punishment?

In general, probably not. It leads to resentment and feeling that the punishment is unfair. The resentment about the punishment might go on long after the crime has been forgotten. If a pre-teenager has done something that costs money to repair, or has stolen money, they should usually pay it back in some way: either by earning through work or through paying out of their pocket money or perhaps in instalments. They will learn best by actually handing over a sum of money to pay for the damaged wall they kicked in, or to replace the money they stole from their mother's purse, even if it's cash they have just received as pocket money.

Should money be given as a reward?

Actually, money is a powerful incentive for good behaviour during pre-teens and teens, and one of the most effective rewards for achievement and effort. There is probably nothing wrong with rewarding your pre-teenager with money from time to time. It is how our society often works. However, money should not be given instead of real parental approval and appreciation. Most pre-teenagers would rather have their parents really proud of them, and showing their approval through their love and appreciation, than just receiving a sum of money. But the money is a real bonus.

The important thing is that regular pocket money or an allowance should be independent from all this, and should not be given as a reward for good behaviour. If it is, there will be storms and fights ahead in their teenage years.

Robert agreed that his family's pocket money arrangement wasn't as bad as he thought, and that he wasn't always making sensible decisions about how he spent his money. 'I have to be able to make my own mistakes though, without my parents going spacko all the time,' he said.

His mother agreed, and said he could suffer in silence if he liked, but she would like to help him do a bit of financial planning. She would give him lunch money once a week and he would agree to eat healthy sandwiches the other days. And what about doing the lawn-mowing, say, once a fortnight?

Self-esteem

'Dear Doctor, I am sending Stephen to see you. He is aged twelve, and isn't coping well with his first year at secondary school. I feel he has low self-esteem and this is affecting his behaviour there.' The letter from Stephen's GP suggested that something was worrying Stephen as he was entering his teenage years, and that it would be worthwhile looking into it now before it became serious.

It was Stephen's mother who worried about his self-esteem. 'He didn't do very well at primary school, even though his father kept on his back to do his homework. I think he isn't really trying at volleyball any more. He wasn't much good at it, but he used to like it. And he's dropped out of scouts.' Apparently his father thought he was just lazy and lacked natural talent for sport.

Stephen's mother was right to worry about what was happening to him, and to question his self-esteem. Stephen's GP was wise in suggesting that something should be done about it before he became an adolescent. Low self-esteem is often blamed for much of the bad behaviour of teenagers. It has been reported that adolescents with low self-esteem are more likely to get into trouble, including abusing alcohol and drugs, and dropping out of school.

Whether this is true or not, it is certainly difficult for children to be happy and grow up successfully if they feel bad about themselves. If they think they are dumb, they may act dumb: what's the point of trying? If they are convinced that they are no good at sport, they will probably stop playing. If they think that they aren't popular with their classmates, they may look for friendships amongst other unsuccessful children like themselves. They may be seen as part of a group of nerds and continue to be put down in the social order amongst their peers.

Yet not all children who aren't bright at schoolwork give up trying at school. Not all children who are uncoordinated, or who lack talent at sport, are unhappy; they may play for fun, even if they don't get in the team. Most children who are not in the top social group at school, and aren't particularly popular, still make good friendships.

And the reverse is just as true. Many teenagers who are really talented at sports eventually stop playing. Many very intelligent students don't reach their potential, and fail at school.

What is self-esteem, and why is it so important?

Self-esteem is how you feel about yourself, how you regard yourself compared to others. It might be how you feel about your body (tall, strong, muscular, slim), your general appearance (good- looking, nice hair, good teeth, nice skin), your physical ability (good at sport, rollerblading, dancing), your social ability (popular, make friends easily), your intelligence (smart at school) and other things you are good at and that you consider important, like art or woodwork.

However, lots of children don't feel good about themselves. Maybe they think that their body is too short, too fat, too skinny or too weak. Perhaps they are convinced that their appearance is ugly, with a wrong-shaped nose, bad skin, too many freckles or horrible hair colour. They may think they are dumb or unpopular, and that no-one wants them as a friend. At puberty, these concerns become even more important. In addition, they may feel bad about their sexual development, such as concern over breast size in girls and penis size in boys.

Self-esteem is established early in childhood, and becomes even more important in the pre-teens, when a child's social outlook starts to expand. When they get into adolescence, self-esteem takes on a whole new social and psychological dimension. Teenagers relate much more to other teenagers, and compare themselves to each other, often to their own disadvantage. They can spend hours checking themselves out in the mirror at home. From a pre-teen or teenage viewpoint, what other teenagers think about them (or what they *think* other teenagers think about them) becomes much more important than what their parents think. The whole problem is made much worse if they get teased, and just about everybody gets teased at some time or another.

It is quite possible, in fact it's very common, to feel bad about some aspect of oneself but good about other aspects. Many overweight children feel bad about their fat body, but otherwise positive about their social ability or their success at schoolwork. A child may know he is not very smart at schoolwork, but if he is good at sport, it may compensate for this. In each case their self-esteem is preserved. But if children feel bad about almost all aspects of themselves, and this starts to make them unhappy, then it becomes important to do something about it. This is when we start to think about poor self-esteem.

Children's views of themselves may not seem logical, and sometimes it is hard to understand where they are coming from. Parents of a child with red hair might think it is the most beautiful colour; but their child might be convinced it is terrible, and that everyone is looking at her and feeling sorry for her. It's not really so bad being a bit shorter than average, and adults know this, but a boy in his pre-teens might think it's a disaster. Some children who think they are fat aren't really fat at all. This doesn't stop them from feeling bad about it. As far as they are concerned, if they think they are fat, they *are* fat.

Self-esteem is gradually developed over many years as children build up a concept of themselves through their perception of what other people think about them.

How does a child develop self-esteem, and how can parents build it up in preparation for the onslaught of the teenage years?

Children develop a concept about themselves in early childhood. They get it from their parents, and later their siblings and other important family members. All of the family contribute to the development of each other's self-esteem. Parents even gain self-esteem from their children, and from the achievement of bringing them up well. Children who get lots of praise when they do good things feel good about it. Children who know that their parents are proud of them tend to feel proud about themselves. This is just as true whether a child has a physical or mental or health problem or not.

Families can help their child develop self-esteem throughout early childhood, and this certainly extends into their pre-teenage years. After this, children increasingly take more note of what their peers say. Teenagers find that it becomes more and more important what other teenagers think of them. Although it will always be important what their parents think and say, it is increasingly hard for them to maintain self-esteem when it is threatened by teenagers and others in their class at school. Of course, as teenagers become more mature, they get things into better perspective, and can judge themselves with less anxiety about what others think. But this may take years.

Self-esteem can be built up during the pre-teen years by finding what things your child is good at, and giving them plenty of praise for it. It's not much good giving them praise for something they are not much good at, even though they may try hard. A child who has achieved something only through very great effort may value praise for their perseverance and need acknowledgment for their achievement, but it may not really boost their self-esteem to be praised for doing something that has taken them a great deal of effort but which other children can do easily and better.

It may be necessary to look for something new for your child to achieve. Perhaps it is a sport he or she hasn't tried yet. There are usually opportunities in the community, if not at school, to try out a new sport or activity. Local councils can often help with information, and you can call them or your local Community Health Centre for advice and contacts.

An activity like dancing or drama will often help a child to gain self-confidence. Drama groups are particularly good at helping children who are hesitant in making friends at school. Acting appeals to most children, and allows shy children to feel more comfortable in relating to others. The same is true for dancing and martial arts like tae kwon do.

Sometimes it is good to do a bit of boasting about your child to relatives and friends, especially in your child's presence. It might test friendships if you do this too much, but grandparents often can't get enough. Enlist their help, because they can support you in developing self-esteem in their grandchild. Anyone who is an important person for a child, whether it is a relative, a teacher or perhaps a friend, can add to a child's development of self-esteem. But parents are the most important.

It is also good for a child to be allowed to fail sometimes

As parents, we can't protect our children from failure all the time. In fact, it isn't always good to succeed in everything. Children need to experience failure sometimes, and in childhood parents can help them overcome disappointments and frustrations. This is probably necessary in preparing them for the adult world and particularly for their teens, when failures and disappointments are inevitable at times. If the pre-teen has never been allowed to fail at something important, it may make it very difficult to experience the day-to-day setbacks that we all have in adult life.

What about Stephen? It turned out that he was great on a BMX bike. His father helped make a track, with the support of the local council, and encouraged him to develop his skills. Soon other children came round to use the track, and Stephen made some new friends who really wanted to be with him. His schoolwork improved a bit, so his father didn't feel he had to be on his back about it all the time, and could concentrate on having fun with him.

Sport and the pre-teenager

Jamie's teenage brother Tom was having a lot of trouble with his knees. His doctor diagnosed a condition which he said affected growing bones. It was not serious, but would limit his sporting activities for a while. The pain certainly did limit his football, and as this was one thing he really excelled at, it was a major blow to him.

The boys' parents wondered whether Tom's involvement in football had started too early. Had his training during his pre-adolescent years been too strenuous? Should they have allowed him to play competition football so young, or waited until he had developed a bit more? 'After all,' they said, 'so many sportsmen seem to end up with knee reconstructions when they are young adults.' They didn't want to make the same mistake with Jamie, who was already showing promise as an athlete and soccer player.

'Another thing,' Jamie's mother said. 'Some of the parents barrack so hard that they spoil the game for many of the children. They seem to live for their children's team success, and abuse the umpire and the opposing players almost worse than at senior league football.'

'The mothers are the worst,' said Tom. 'Some of the kids get a really bad time after the match if they lose.'

'It's supposed to be for the kids, but sometimes you'd think it was really for the parents,' said their mother. 'I think the important thing is to play and have fun, not just to win.'

'Yeah, but it's still good to win,' said Tom.

'It's only a game, after all.'

'Try telling that to the coach!' said Tom and Jamie together.

Sport is fun (or it should be)

Sport is fun. Sport is good for pre-teens and teenagers. Sport provides physical activity that keeps them fit. Team sports give a sense of belonging to a group, which children at this age find so important for their social development. Sport can provide a challenge, and then there comes the pride in participation and a sense of achievement. Success in sport (not necessarily in winning, but in doing well) boosts self-esteem. Sport provides a topic for conversation between friends and in the family. Parents like to watch their children play sport: it is something that they can feel proud about. Sport is something to look forward to, to work towards, to train for and to make you feel happy.

If all this is true, as it is for most pre-teens and teenagers, why don't all children play sport? How could there be any possible harm in it? Isn't it a responsibility for schools to provide sporting facilities?

Schools usually do encourage sport for children, especially as they enter their teens. They do it for various reasons: to encourage fitness, to aid personal development, to work off surplus energy and to help bonding within the school community.

Most pre-teenagers aren't very fit

Some years ago an inquiry into the health of schoolchildren showed some rather surprising results in measurements of physical fitness. Not only were Australian school children not very fit, they were even less fit than American school children. The notion of Australia being a nation of fit, sporting young people didn't seem to hold up in surveys of our youth, any more than it would for adults.

These findings led to physical education being placed firmly back on the curriculum in many schools. In primary schools this usually meant noncompetitive physical activities like running and active games in the regular school timetable. As these fail to hold the interest of older children, competitive sport becomes increasingly important in providing physical activity.

Sport is often the most enjoyable way for pre-teenagers to keep fit, but some schools are concerned that any competition in sport leads to a 'winners and losers' mentality. This means that some will fail, and some schools feel that failure is bad for children. So they are often not encouraged to try hard by competing against each other. The concept of 'beating your personal best' may work well for many adults, but it doesn't spur many pre-teenagers to achieve their full potential unless there are also the exciting rewards provided by competitive sport.

Physical activity is good for pre-teenagers

All parents know this. It isn't always possible for them to provide the opportunities for activity and encouragement their pre-teenagers may need. When both parents work there isn't much time to take children to play outside or visit sporting grounds; TV becomes a necessary alternative recreation. Families living in busy streets or in flats may also have difficulty in letting their pre-teenagers loose in the neighbourhood to get exercise. So it may have to be up to schools.

Unfortunately some schools are finding that resources and priorities limit the physical education programme, and this has become quite a problem in some secondary schools. Is physical fitness the responsibility of schools? Should sport compete with maths? In most schools, it is accepted that physically active children are more likely to benefit from the whole education programme than those who are not active. A healthy body and a healthy mind are said to go together. Whether this is really true, of course, would be hard to prove. Lots of children who have health problems that limit their physical ability still do well academically.

For most children as they enter their pre-teens it is probably true that a physically active child is more likely to be healthy and happy.

What about competitive sport?

There is a difference between physical activity and competitive sport. Competitive sport often means intensive training, pushing young people to their physical limits. The competition may mean not only competing with the opposite side or other competitors, but also a fierce struggle to get into a team ahead of friends. Team managers and coaches often have to put up with reproaches, and even abuse, from parents of a child who is left out of a team. Children who don't make the team may feel shattered and ashamed.

Competitive sport doesn't suit everyone, and choosing the right sport for a pre-teenager may make all the difference between success and failure, happiness and unhappiness.

What are the some of the possible harmful effects from sport at this age?

INJURIES
Bones and joints are more vulnerable to stress and injury during periods of rapid growth. Growth is relatively slow in the pre-teenage years, preceding the rapid growth spurt of adolescence. This rapid growth spurt occurs rather late in puberty in boys, though it happens earlier in girls; and in both girls and boys this doesn't normally occur until the teenage years. So pre-teenagers are often

growing rather slowly. For this reason, injuries to knees and ankles from sport tend to be less common in pre-teenagers than teenagers.

Another factor is that sport is usually more supervised, and often less physically demanding, at this age. The risk of injuries can be reduced by proper preparation for the sport and adequate warm-up before the game. Injuries are more likely to occur if the pre-teenager is overstressed and tired.

GROWTH

It has been shown that pre-teenagers who engage in prolonged and intensive training programmes may have impaired growth and delayed puberty development. This seems to be a particular risk for girl gymnasts and ballet students. It is sometimes accompanied by an inadequate food intake, perhaps in the belief that a very slim figure enhances performance. Perhaps it does for some activities, but there may be a physical price to pay. Those pre-teenagers who combine intense training with dieting certainly run the risk of physical harm with impaired growth.

On the other hand, moderate physical exercise through sport may actually enhance growth.

EXCEEDING LIMITS OF ENDURANCE

It has been suggested that endurance sports, like cross-country running, should have limitations set for each age group, based on the physical development of most children of that age. There is the risk that an overenthusiastic coach may push his or her athletes too far. Whether or not there should be an actual limitation on the distances, or degree of effort, in a sporting activity pre-teenagers should not exceed their level of fitness.

In the pre-teenage years there is a rather wide variation of physical development according to whether puberty has started or not. This should (but often doesn't) lead to consideration of the individual abilities of the pre-teenager, rather than their age. Some studies on sport for children have suggested that the most important thing is for coaches to ensure proper preparation for the sport, rather than setting limits for each age. Graduated training, proper warm-up, and not allowing a child to go beyond their own physical limits will minimise any harm that might come from prolonged or intense endurance sports.

At the end of a run (or any other sporting activity) the pre-teenager should not be in pain or feel totally exhausted and worn out. They may be tired, but they should feel good after sport. This means that the activity hasn't been excessive for them.

Sport for pre-teenagers with a chronic health problem

Most children with a chronic illness or disability will benefit from doing sport to their own capacity, for all the reasons that other children benefit, but also for social reasons and to maintain a positive attitude to health. Children with asthma should discuss this with their doctor, but with adequate preventative medication and available treatment medication if they get wheezy (plus some other precautions) they will almost certainly benefit from sport. Pre-teenagers with diabetes can do virtually all sports (except scuba diving) but they may need to make adjustments in insulin and food intake. Obese pre-teenagers may feel embarrassed to wear sports clothes or undress publicly, or they may feel they would be too slow or not get picked for a team. They should still participate, as sport may play an important part in developing a good figure and controlling weight. It may be a matter of choosing the right sport.

Psychological effects

Most of the psychological effects of sport are positive. Just being part of a group playing sport, whether they play well or not, and whether they win or not, is great. Winning is a bonus, and everyone needs to win sometimes. Having fun and keeping fit may be the best outcome, and doing this makes for happiness. Pre-teenagers are herd animals. They thrive in company, and sport is a good way to be having fun in a group, or just participating with one or two friends.

The trouble is that if these things don't happen, the pre-teenager can feel very put down. Failure to get picked for a team, or being blamed for letting the side down, can be devastating. Sometimes a pre-teenager feels that they are just no good at sport, and stop trying. Maybe they are not very coordinated, and don't get into the cricket team, but could do well at cross-country running or rowing. I have known some boys, who had no aptitude for sport, get enormous satisfaction in being a linesman or scoring for the team. That way they were still part of the group.

What can parents do to ensure that their pre-teenager gets the most out of sport?

Encourage your child to try, even if they are not very robust or good at sport. Sports teachers at school can usually involve everyone in ways that all pre-teens can enjoy and feel part of the group.

Try to involve your pre-teenager in a sport that they can enjoy and do well. There are many opportunities now in local clubs, and many schools offer options that cater for very different abilities.

Make sure that your pre-teenager is involved in a sport that is properly supervised. If it is physically demanding, make sure that training is appropriate. Sometimes junior coaches are good at encouraging participation and developing skills, but less experienced in preparing young people for demanding sporting achievement.

Be careful not to allow your pre-teenager to become so involved in sport that it intrudes on other social and school activities. There may come a time in their teenage years when your child will show so much talent and enthusiasm that you will want to help him or her to become really outstanding. At their pre-teens, however, it is usually wise to encourage them to keep their options open, in case they sacrifice too much in the hope of success, or to please parents or their coach. This seems to be a particular risk in swimming and other sports requiring a combination of physical skills and endurance training.

Show them that you are proud of them if they get picked for a team, and go to watch them play if you can. This is especially important for fathers and sons. It is also important for pre-teenagers who aren't quite so good at sport as a successful brother or sister. *'Dad never comes to watch me play. He only goes to watch Pam, because she's really good and I'm pretty hopeless.'* In fact Dad may watch his elder daughter, Pam, because she needs to be driven to her events, or because her team plays when he's free to watch. But pre-teenagers don't always see it that way.

Don't get too involved in their success or failure. If you do, they may give up if they don't think they are living up to your expectations.

What about Jamie and Tom? Their mother recognised that Tom's knee problems were a reflection on his age and enthusiasm for the physical demands of his football. It was most unlikely that his involvement in football in his pre-teens had caused the problem. But she was going to watch Jamie more closely as he developed his talents at sport, and encourage him to have as much fun as he could.

Fathers ... who needs them?

Joe was only twelve and had already run away from home twice. The first time he hadn't gone far, because it was late at night and he didn't know where to go. He was found by his mother and her new partner hiding near the park (and probably Joe really wanted to be found). The next time he had taken his rollerblades and managed to go 15 kilometres without arousing much attention from anyone. He eventually turned up at his father's flat at 2 a.m. He begged his father (who was astonished to see him) not to tell his mother he was there, at least until the morning, so he could spend the night with his dad.

'I didn't really know what to do,' his father told me next day. 'In the end, he was so cold and tired and sad, I just cuddled him and we both cried and he fell asleep; so I let him stay. I knew if I rang his mother she would have been round with the police straight away. So I rang her in the morning, first thing.'

It was clear that Joe and his father hadn't been together much for a long time, and they were missing each other. Joe was certainly missing his dad, and also possibly troubled that his mother was starting a new relationship with a man who she said would be a new father for him.

'David's all right, I suppose,' Joe told me when we met with his father later that day. 'But he's always around, and Mum seems to spend all her time with him. And sometimes they argue just like she did with my real father, and it's about me all the time. And anyway, he's not my dad.'

The incident had helped Joe's father rethink his relationship with his son, who was nearing his teenage years. 'I had always felt very close to Joe. We have so many common interests, and I love his company. But after his mother and I split up four years ago, I haven't seen much of him. At first, I used to see him regularly, but his mother said that every time he came home after spending a day with me, he behaved so badly; it obviously wasn't good for him to be with me at all. I couldn't really argue, because she had custody.'

Joe's mother came to see me later that week. She was furious with her ex-husband. 'He wasn't much of a father when we were together,' she told me. 'Always working late, and when he got home he drank, and could be quite violent. We had terrible fights and I decided it was best for Joe if we separated. Now I've got a new partner. I was hoping everything would settle down and Joe would have a new stepfather for when he is a teenager.'

What made her even more upset was the fact that she had looked after Joe all these years — put up with his difficult behaviour, coped when he was sick — and now he seemed to want his father.

'He never showed much interest in the boy up till now,' she said. 'Just cards and phone calls for his birthday and at Christmas. The presents he sent were often unsuitable and I sometimes had to send them back.'

Fathers aren't always close to their children during their pre-teens

Even fathers in stable families often leave most of the task of rearing the children to their mother, and may seem to show only passing interest in their growing children's problems and difficulties. They may be ready enough to have fun with their children when everyone is in a good mood, but become impatient when things are going wrong. They may be quick to punish children when they misbehave in their presence, but they usually aren't around at the critical times for bad behaviour such as after school, when there are arguments about television and about whose turn it is for the computer. They often don't hear about the many times when the pre-teenagers are asked to do chores around the house and they argue, and put it off, until they drive their mother mad, then accuse her of nagging.

Sometimes fathers are given the task of discipline, or at least are made to share it. 'Just wait till your father gets home!' and 'Do something about your son!' hardly makes for a peaceful homecoming for the father. If it happens too often, it hardly makes for a warm relationship between the father and his pre-teenager. Mothers, on the other hand, are usually the ones that children turn to when they have a problem or they feel sick.

Sometimes fathers just don't seem to have enough time to listen to their children when they want to talk about worries and problems. By their pre-teens, boys often feel uncomfortable in discussing personal matters and emotional feelings with their father. They may feel that it isn't acting like a man to show sadness or cry, or it may seem like weakness to share their feelings with their father. Even mothers might not get to hear about some private and emotional things that a pre-teenager may feel ashamed about. Then they might not be able to tell anyone.

So sometimes fathers aren't very close to their children, even when they get on well together. They might go to watch them play sport, and might go to parent–teacher interviews at school to hear about how well (or badly) their child is doing, and about misbehaviour in class. But they might still find it hard to talk together about things that are really important to either of them. They might not really understand just how their child is growing up emotionally in the pre-teenage period. And if that is so, it could be a lot harder later on when they are in their teenage years.

It's a lot harder for absent fathers

When parents find that their marriage can't continue and decide to separate, it is usual for younger children to stay with their mother. Fathers may seem to be expendable, and even if the marriage ends amicably and with the children's interest paramount and reasonable access arrangements, fathers somehow often get pushed into the background.

Things might go reasonably well for a while, and although there may be some problems with arrangements (especially if an access weekend coincides with a friend's birthday party) absent fathers may get on quite well with their children on an arrangement that gives them reasonable time together on a regular basis.

Four things could make it more difficult for the father–son or father–daughter relationship, unless both parents make great effort to help their child.

1. The father makes a new relationship, and perhaps gets married. So much depends on how the child's mother views this new development. Was the new partner the one responsible for the break-up in the marriage in the first place? Is she trying to take over some of the mother's role when their child visits? Does the new relationship put the father's interest in his children at a lower priority, or are maintenance payments at risk?

    What if the father's new partner doesn't really like the children for some reason, or feels threatened by them? Or if she tries to like them, but they don't accept her and make her life a misery? Perhaps she has standards of behaviour and expectations that undermine the children's real mother's standards. She may let them stay up late, or she may smoke and allow them to try, or perhaps make them do an unreasonable amount of chores around her house.

Sometimes the children have always nurtured a hope that their estranged parents might come together again one day, however much they are told this is impossible. Then a new partner in either of their parent's lives might destroy their hopes for the reconciliation they had wanted so much. It wouldn't be surprising if sometimes a pre-teenager actually tried to sabotage the new relationship in the irrational belief that it might restore hope that his or her parents would reunite.

2.　Their mother finds a new partner. Similar problems may result. The new partner might be very careful not to usurp the role of parent, but when there are the usual arguments between mother and pre-teenager, it might be hard not to intervene. The inevitable 'You're not my father' response hurts everyone.

Sometimes the new partner or stepfather does try to assume the role of the father, and if he is accepted as such, this may be good for the new family arrangements. The stepfather may be very understanding and helpful to the pre-teenager who is looking for a male role model. But it can still be very confusing for pre-teenagers who may have difficulty in working out complex relationships, and if the real father is around he may feel pushed further away from his children. It can be very hard for a father to see someone else living with his children, playing with them, watching over them, enjoying their company and guiding their development. Some fathers respond to this by moving further away from their children so as not to get too hurt by constant reminders of this exclusion from their children's lives.

3.　The pre-teenager's mother puts their father down, either consciously or unconsciously. She may complain about his meagre maintenance payments, or apparent lack of interest in his children. She may remember aloud some of the difficult times they had together before they separated, and especially if he drank, or was violent, or was unfaithful. This is especially confusing for a pre-teenage boy, who usually has a strong desire to be approved of by his father and needs to look up to him.

4.   The pre-teenager may decide he or she would rather live with their father. Perhaps this is because of the rows and fights that have happened with their mother. Perhaps a boy longs to be closer to his father as he enters his early years of puberty. It's worse if the pre-teen behaves so badly that their mother agrees to let them live with their father but it then turns out that their father can't cope with them, or his partner doesn't want them around. Then the pre-teen may return home, hurt by their apparent failure to be with their father, and confused by a situation where they don't seem to be wanted by either parent.

How could this all be prevented?

Whether families are living together or not, as the children are approaching their teenage years it is a good time for fathers to become even more involved in their children's development. It is time for both parents to discuss how the change from childhood to adolescence may lead to a change in relationships within the family. It affects both the mother and the father, but it is often the father who has to make adjustments and reconsider his role within the family. His role during this phase of the children's lives becomes important in helping to set standards of behaviour, in making rules and keeping the peace through mediation in the inevitable disagreements within the family. He can *not* leave all this to the children's mother.

He will be essential in supporting his daughters and sons in their passage through puberty. Daughters need to trust their father, and to learn from him the ways adult men can be depended on to support and care for others. His active involvement in his son's development will be critical in a different way. Sons need their father as an adult role model. If a father lets his children down at this time, it will make it very much harder for them to learn trust and responsibility as adults.

Perhaps the father could take a greater role in making the rules and helping to make them stick. If he hasn't done so previously, he could go to the parent–teacher interviews to understand his pre-teenager better, and to demonstrate his interest in their progress. He could ask himself whether more of his leisure time should be spent with his children, now that they are getting older. He could make sure that there is time for having fun together. Many fathers enjoyed playing with their children when they were toddlers, but seemed to drift away from them when work became more demanding, or their children developed friendships and interests outside the home.

What do pre-teenage boys need from their father?

Children of all ages need their parents for various reasons. Most can grow up well as small children with the main care from just one parent (usually their mother), but as they approach their teens the roles of each parent may change, and many of the needs of boys at this age are different from that of girls.

Some of the needs that teenage boys express over and over again, in various ways, about their father are obvious enough. Many fathers may feel confident they are meeting those needs, even though their son may not think so. Sometimes boys deny that they want their fathers to be involved in their lives, even though subconsciously they really do. Sometimes boys become angry that their father seems uninterested in them, and protect their pride by saying that they don't care.

Here are some of the ways that boys need their father at this age.

TO FOSTER A SENSE OF BELONGING

Pre-teenagers have a great need to belong to their family (at the very time that they seem to be moving away from it), and their relationship with their father may be critical. *'My dad'* can have great meaning for a boy: there is a sense of possession, of pride in their relationship, and a sense of being a son. When families split up, and there is a stepfather at home and a biological father somewhere else, *'My real dad'* has special meaning for some boys.

TO BE A ROLE MODEL

All pre-teenagers need role models. Boys look to their father as an adult same-sex role model as they enter their pre-teen and teenage years, and they start to work out what sort of person they are. Mothers cannot do this for their teenage sons, even though they may instil morals and standards of behaviour that will stand their children in good stead throughout their lives. For good or bad, boys at this age tend to emulate their father, unless their relationship is so bad that that the boy rejects his father as someone worthy enough to admire. If fathers don't provide a role model, the pre-teenager may find another adult who will; they may feel so estranged from their father that they will emulate stars from bands or TV.

TO BE PROUD OF THEM

Boys need their father to be proud of them. It raises and sustains their fragile self-esteem. It reinforces good behaviour and endeavour. It strengthens the bond that exists between them.

TO HAVE FUN WITH THEM

Relationships between father and son are strongest if they have fun together. This goes beyond doing things together as a family. It may mean just enjoying each other's company when the rest of the family are doing something else. It may mean going to a sporting event or concert together. It may mean a boy helping his father by doing work on the car or in the garage. It may mean helping with a hobby (either the father's or the son's).

When I ask pre-teen and teenage boys what they would like to do with a father they hardly ever see, the three most common things they think of are going camping, going fishing and going to the football together. Sometimes they would like to bring along one or two mates, but often they just want to have fun with their father. The sad thing is that if fathers are too busy at this age, their son may lose interest, and find other ways to have fun. Then it is the father who has missed out, as much as his son.

TO TEACH THEM THINGS

Boys like to learn things from their fathers, even things that their mother could teach them perfectly well. In many parts of the world (and even in industrialised countries this is sometimes true), boys expect to follow their father's trade or occupation. So they learn about the land, or about a craft or a profession. Fathers were always an important part of their children's education. Now that schools have largely taken over this role, fathers need to recognise that their sons can really benefit from their experience, skills and interests, even though they probably won't be following their career.

TO HELP THEM EXPLORE ADULT RELATIONSHIPS

Even though teenagers learn a lot about relationships from each other, what they learn isn't always very mature or responsible. Fathers can help both their sons and their daughters to develop a sense of responsibility towards other people. They can show the importance of trust and reliance in each other. This paves the ways to caring for other people, and ultimately to a successful long-term relationship when they are older (and ready for it).

So it is a good idea to start linking up fathers and sons at the pre-teenage years. If they are together at home as an intact family, this may be relatively easy. It may just take some thought and planning. For families who have separated, the relationship with a boy's (and girl's) natural father may need to be strengthened or re-examined. Stepfathers may have to take a greater role in some families. It's all part of helping a pre-teenager to enter their teens comfortably.

What do pre-teenage daughters need from their father?

The emphasis has been on the special needs that boys have for their father, because it is usually the boys who miss out most when fathers are too busy to be involved with their family, or if the parents have separated. It is often the boys who demonstrate their distress through bad behaviour or failing to achieve at school.

But daughters also need their father at this age. They need them for all the reasons discussed above. They especially need their father's love and respect. They need to be valued by both parents, and want their father to be proud of their achievements while they are growing up.

Fathers have a responsibility in helping their daughters to understand men. It would be hard to learn this from their mother, or from their brothers, or the soaps, and they certainly won't learn from immature teenage boys at school. It will be helpful for her to appreciate the role of men within families. Fathers have a responsibility to show that men can be supportive and can be trusted in a relationship. It is very sad when fathers can't provide these needs both by example and through a loving relationship with their daughter.

What about Joe? His mother ended up feeling relieved that his father was prepared to take more interest in him, as Joe wasn't helping her own relationship with her new partner, David. She let Joe stay overnight with his father and go away for a holiday with him. Eventually, about a year later, Joe decided to live with his father, but he was still seeing his mother regularly, and their relationship improved. He even liked being with Peter when he visited his mother, and accepted him as a stepfather.

TV, videos and computer games

'*It's amazing, Doctor. He can spend hours playing on his computer. Everything else gets forgotten. If we try to call him for meals he just shouts 'In a minute' and still doesn't come. Homework gets put off, and the biggest fights amongst our children are when someone wants a game when the other is using it. It's not as if he's actually learning anything from the wretched computer games.'*

'*Yes I am, Mum,' Eric interrupted his concentration in his hand-held game for a moment. 'I learn quick reflexes and hand coordination, my dad says.'*

'*Well that's about all, and it's driving me mad. And there was nothing wrong with your quick reflexes or your hand coordination in the first place. I'll check out mine on you soon if you don't stop.'*

Earlier that day a mother was discussing her worry that her twelve-year-old was spending so much time watching television. It was also getting in the way of homework and often family meals were spread out between the TV room and the kitchen if there was a favourite show on. TV and videos and computer games are here to stay, but can they cause harm, and should there be limits set?

The answer is probably yes, they can be harmful; and yes, if you think that your pre-teen is too preoccupied with them there should be limits set and firm rules made and kept.

What are the potential harmful effects?

THEY CAN INTERFERE WITH A GROWING CHILD'S NEED FOR EXERCISE AND PHYSICAL ACTIVITY

If a TV show is more attractive after school than going outside and playing with friends, or riding a bike, it should be rationed.

Some children are naturally active, and need no encouragement to go off with friends. Some are naturally inactive and miss the exercise if there is a soft option like the TV.

There have been some research studies suggesting that too many hours a day in front of a TV may increase the risk to a child to get fat. Certainly if a child is overweight, watching TV for hours instead of burning up energy outside will make it very difficult to control excess weight.

THEY CAN GET IN THE WAY OF ORDINARY FAMILY LIFE AND ROUTINE
TV shows can take precedence over things that families do together (such as chores and games and meals) and thus deprive family members of social interaction and from talking, to the others. It's tough on mother or father if they want to tell the family what a hard day they've had, or on the children if something interesting or funny happened at school. Meals can be good family social times, but it's harder to talk intelligently to anyone if the TV's on! Even if everyone is watching a programme, there's hardly much opportunity for real family discussion. No wonder so many teenagers say that no-one ever listens to them.

TV CAN PUT A CHILD'S MIND IN A RATHER PASSIVE MODE
Unlike reading or doing things, where there is scope for imagination and active thought, and talking, where there is interaction and scope for the development of ideas, TV fully occupies the mind and leaves little for the child's intelligence to dwell on. This effect can continue for hours after the show is over, and is not a helpful frame of mind for homework.

TV also tends to present information in very small bits. Producers have recognised that most viewers' attention for news or public affairs is a matter of a few minutes. Children can get very interested in learning about things, but they may find difficulty in maintaining concentration if they get used to the way television presents information. Some people think that TV is a good way to learn about the world, and it can be, but not the way it is usually presented on entertainment TV.

Computer games can be addictive

Some children, especially pre-teens, get hooked on them. They seem to need to spend more and more time on games, and need more and more new ones. This is one reason why computer games have been so successful. They capture the attention of even those children who have very short attention spans and poor concentration for anything else. This reaction is partly because there is a quick response to every move the player makes, and each move leads to something else. It also keeps the fingers busy, with an obvious and immediate response. It puts the player in control; if they make a mistake, they can always start again.

Is all this a bad thing? Perhaps not, but it could be if the games seem to preoccupy the pre-teenager's mind, in the same way that any other addiction can. Then the games can become more important than other things, like learning and family interaction. Games can also be a rather poor means to overcome boredom, loneliness or depression in a pre-teenager. If your child seems to be spending too much time on computer or video games, it might be worthwhile considering these possibilities.

Eric's mother decided that as he was doing well at his first year at high school, and he seemed to be a lively and entertaining child who could switch off his computer games if something better was on offer, she didn't need to worry about him. However, she decided that the games couldn't intrude on family chores or homework, and Eric would have to stick to the rules. He agreed.

Talking to Your pre-teenager

Get into the habit of listening to them before they decide it's not worth talking to you

'You never listen to me.' Linda was talking away to her mother, who in turn was telling me that she never listened to what she was telling her to do.

'What do you mean, I never listen to you? You talk all the time. Shouting is more like it. And anyway, I never know if you are telling the truth and you just argue and argue and argue. Sometimes you give me a headache. I notice you don't talk to your father like that.'

'No, well, he's never home, is he? Or he's too busy.'

'He wouldn't stand for the language you use to me.'

'Like what? Just because I call you a …'

I thought it was a good time to stop this argument before I learnt more about Linda's vocabulary of abusive terms she used for her mother.

It's fun listening to young children. They like to tell you what they did, saw or are going to do. They like entertaining you, and sharing with you all the amazing and funny things they have thought about. They can easily charm you with their stories and the things that have interested them. When they are a little older, they want to tell you about things that have upset them.

When they are teenagers, however, they might not feel comfortable about telling their parents (or anyone else, for that matter) about the things that really worry them or that occupy so much of their developing mind. They might think parents wouldn't understand or, would think they were stupid, or it might be embarrassing. If they had a very worrying problem, they might not want to add to their parents' own problems by distressing them with their pre-teen concerns. Not sensible, perhaps, but that's how many teenagers think.

Being a pre-teenager is a phase in childhood development in which children can still feel comfortable about sharing their thoughts and worries with their parents. It's a gradual process from telling you about the things they have seen and done, to telling you about the things that are on their mind, or that are going wrong.

Pre-teens don't always pick the best time to tell you about important things that are on their mind. They might want to talk to you when you are coping with the baby, or with a toddler who is demanding attention (so you will be rather preoccupied and the pre-teenager will decide that you are only interested in their brother or sister, and not in them). Maybe you are tired, or have other things on your mind, and the pre-teenager picks that very time to tell you something they think important, even if you don't.

Sometimes they will just drop little hints and expect you to work out what it is that it is important to them. They may be trying to say that they want to discuss something with you, but are not quite sure how to start. *'Mum, I couldn't understand what the teacher was saying about fractions today'* could mean *'I wonder if I'm dumb'* or *'That teacher is mean to me'* or *'The kids were teasing me during maths and I got the blame and got sent out of class so I missed the bit about fractions'*.

Of course, it could have just meant *'Could you please help me understand my maths'*. Perhaps the right response would be, if you were too busy, *'Get your dad to explain it to you when he gets home because I'm too busy right now'*. But if it was meant as an opening to talk about one of the other things on their mind, and you didn't respond (or you put it off) you may have missed an opportunity to discuss how your child felt about their schoolwork or their relationship with the teacher. And they might have got the feeling that you aren't really interested in their worries, or don't really want to be bothered listening to them.

Most pre-teenagers will be prepared to let you put off the discussion for a little time if they think you really want to hear about their worries, and are prepared to listen later. But not too much later. The teenager, on the other hand, often won't let you come back to discuss something in your own time. *'If you won't talk about it right now when it is important to me and on my mind, forget it.'* Be prepared for this, because parents sometimes miss opportunities to hear about really worrying things altogether.

If you listen to the pre-teen as they tell you about whatever's on their mind, even if it's inconvenient to spare the time, they will think it's worthwhile telling you about important things. They may not seem very important things to you, but they could be to them. They get into the habit of telling you about worries, and not just the things that they think that you want to hear.

Sometimes just listening is enough, and you don't have to come up with solutions to the problems. For a pre-teenager, talking something through, and knowing that their parent understands how they feel, is often enough to make a problem less worrying. You may need to prompt the discussion with questions or guesses. *'That must have made you feel pretty mad.' 'Did you feel he was being unfair?' 'Is she being mean to other kids too, or just to you?'*

Of course, pre-teens do need, and want, advice and guidance. That is one of the roles of parents, teachers and other adults whom the pre-teenager trusts and respects. Practical solutions and suggestions may resolve many worries. There is a lot that pre-teens have to worry about: sharing a problem and talking through possible solutions will help a lot.

On the other hand, a 'discussion' often really means that the pre-teen does the talking and the parent does the listening. This could be quite a new experience for a child, who is so used to being talked at, and expected to do the listening. It could be exasperating for the parent, who may be longing to tell their child what to do and get on with it. Persevere — it's well worthwhile. It sets the stage for good communication when teenage arrives.

What do they mean when they say ... ?

'I dunno'

This often means 'I don't want to talk about it'. It's meant to make it difficult for you to pursue questions like 'What's the matter with you?' or 'Why did you get such a bad school report?' or 'How did the cupboard door get broken?' or 'Who ate the cake in the fridge I was keeping for visitors?' When they say ' I dunno' they mean 'Don't ask me because I don't know, and I certainly don't want to talk about it, so it's a waste of your time and mine to discuss it at all'.

But you know they probably really do know, and they want to keep it to themselves. Pre-teens learn that owning up to something often leads to a big row, so it's better to maintain their innocence by professing ignorance. Sometimes of course they really don't know the answer to questions like 'Why did you hit your brother?' or 'Where are your sports clothes?'

'What are you thinking about?' 'Nothing'

Nothing may be exactly what they *are* thinking about. Pre-teenagers daydream a lot sometimes. It's restful and doesn't take much effort, especially when you are supposed to be doing your schoolwork. After all, some people who teach relaxation therapy ask you to clear your mind and think about a colour or something equally empty. Some kids can do that without even trying, let alone taking lessons.

'What are you doing?' 'Nothing' may mean just that; but beware, it may be the only answer they can think of when they are doing something bad and they hope you won't find out about it.

There is a problem here for parents. If you challenge pre-teens too vigorously, or push them too far, they may think up more convincing ways of deceiving you. As they get into their teens (and become less naive) they get better and better at it. Sometimes it's better to let them know that you're not deceived, but don't challenge them or put them down too much at the time, especially in front of friends or siblings. You can always come back to the misdeed later, when they are calm and receptive to being admonished. After all, none of us likes to be called a liar, even when we have been lying.

'It wasn't me'

This probably doesn't mean anything at all. All children in families say this. It can become a chorus. There are lots of variations, like 'Don't look at me', 'Don't ask me' and, if they want to be aggressive and appear innocent, 'What are you asking me for?' or better still, 'Stop picking on me, will you?'

'I hate you'

This means 'Right now I'm very angry with you, and I know a good way to upset you is to tell you that I hate you, because that will really hurt'. And it's better than kicking you. Of course, they really mean it at the time, but it doesn't mean anything more than anger, or perhaps frustration, at not getting what they want.

It's more a worry if they tell you that they hate someone in the family at a time when there isn't some obvious reason, like a fight in progress or if they have just lost an argument. It might be worthwhile sitting down and talking about it. It isn't always very helpful to dismiss 'I hate him' by saying 'Of course you don't' or 'Don't say anything so horrible about your big brother' or even 'Your father really loves you, you know'. If you have time to listen, you might be able to work out what it was that that person has done, (or seems to have done) that led to your pre-teen telling you that they hate them. They may be just sounding off at some perceived insult or injustice, but it could be a way of saying that something is really wrong, and asking for help.

'Go away' and 'Leave me alone'

They may mean 'I'm upset and I want to sulk'. A bit of a cuddle may still help a miserable pre-teen. Make the most of the pre-teen years to show them that you understand that they have feelings and sometimes express them in ways that seem to exclude parents. Don't be offended; they may be starting to work out emotional problems for themselves, but they probably still need your help. When they become teenagers they will probably really mean what they say, and reject any effort you may make to comfort or help them, particularly if you didn't seem to try much when they were younger.

'Why do you always pick on me?'

This particular question doesn't call for an answer of 'I don't', even if you don't pick on them any more than they deserve. When you think about it, perhaps you do find that you pick on them rather a lot at times. Perhaps you expect a bit much of them now that they seem so much bigger and grown-up. They might do a lot of irritating things, and you haven't had time to work out why. The bigger they are, the more annoying they can be (and it could get worse: wait till they are bigger than you!). Try to sort things out now, because when they become teenagers they can get impossible to reason with if they think you have been unfair.

'It's not fair'

Sometime in their pre-teen years, children work out that life isn't always fair. People get sick or die, and it isn't their fault. You can get punished for something you didn't do, or perhaps your punishment was too severe. Other kids have things that you haven't. Your older brother can stay up later than you, or watch something on TV that you can't. You can't have a rabbit as a pet, even though you've seen just the one you really want at the pet shop and you promise to clean out its cage and get cabbage leaves for it each week and you've always wanted a rabbit and Robert has a cat so why can't you anyway ...

Life *is* unfair. It's a hard lesson to learn, but it's better to find it out while you are a pre-teen and can talk about it with your parents. Teenagers who haven't had that chance may rebel against what they feel is unfair. They may do so in ways that hurt themselves and others.

'It's not my fault'

Actually, it probably *is* ! Or partly, anyway. Pre-teens have to learn to take responsibility for what they have done, and acknowledge mistakes they have made. It's a valuable lesson, and best learnt during the pre-teen years when parents can reason with them, and they will listen and respect your advice. In their teenage years, if they haven't learnt this lesson, they might become very resentful about taking blame for something they have done. They will find other people to take the blame. 'The other kids started it.' 'You never give me enough money, so I have to steal it.' 'You're worse than me: look what Dad does.' 'He deserved it' (when they have just beaten somebody up). 'It's society's fault, not mine.' Sometimes these attitudes of not accepting responsibility for what they do can persist into adult life.

'Don't nag all the time'

I usually tell pre-teens that mothers are supposed to nag: if they don't, they may not be doing a good job. They usually agree. 'Yeah, but not as bad as my mum.' Then they might even be willing to discuss strategies to help their mothers kick their bad nagging habit, like putting their dirty clothes in the laundry.

'I'm no good'

The trouble is that this may be a self-fulfiling prophecy. The more a pre-teen thinks that they are no good, the more they are likely to *be* no good. Several years ago a group of researchers put this to the test. They told a group of children that they were doing a study to see how accurately children could throw a ball. One group were told that they had been picked out because the teachers said they were the best. Another were told they were the weak, hopeless group, but the researchers wanted to see if that was correct, so please try as hard as you can. Of course, no-one had actually identified the children that way, it was just part of the research. Anyway, the group who had been told they were the best actually proved much more accurate in the ball-throwing tests than the group who thought they had been identified as hopeless.

In the next part of the experiment, the researchers told the weak group that they had been wrong, and actually this group were better than the other group, and they would like them to do the ball throwing again to show everyone how good they really were. This time they performed just as well as the group who *thought* they were the best. So, the lesson was that if children think they good at something, they will do much better at it than if they think they are not much good.

We need to take it seriously when pre-teens say that they are no good, in case they give up trying. This is just as true even if we don't agree with them, we actually think that they are quite good. When they get to their teens, they often give up completely, because adolescents hate to fail in front of each other. With pre-teens, it's not too late to find out what things they *are* good at, and encourage them to develop their ability in those things. If they really aren't much good at something, such as sport or maths, it's worth working out why, and helping them to improve. Perhaps some remedial gym or special coaching may help. Even with this extra help, they will need a lot of encouragement to counteract the negative feelings they may have about themselves.

'I don't care'

Pre-teens (and teens) often say this as a strategy to protect themselves from getting hurt any more than they already are. If something has gone wrong, and they do care about it, it hurts. So, if they don't get picked for the footy team, they might say they don't care. If the homework is too difficult and doesn't get done, they might say they don't care. If someone they thought was their best friend doesn't ask them to her birthday party, it helps if they say they don't care. Like all such strategies, this one helps to protect feelings, and it probably doesn't help to challenge them by arguing that they really do care. It may be better to understand that there could be a problem underlying the 'I don't care', and tackle that if you can.

'There's no homework to do tonight'

Unlikely as this may be, this might just possibly mean that there *is* no homework to do tonight. If it's a recurring theme (and particularly if the school report says that homework isn't always handed in) it could mean: 'I left it in my locker at school'; 'I don't want do it and you can't make me if I say there isn't any'; 'I have something better to watch on TV'; 'I am finding it too hard to settle down to do the homework at night'; 'I have lost my school diary again'; 'I am doing so badly at school that I can't understand my homework (and you can't help me)'; 'Things are so unhappy for me at school that doing homework just extends the unhappiness'; 'I lost what the teacher handed out to do'; 'If I hand in my homework every day, my friends will think I am a geek'.

Parents often think that their pre-teen is trying it on when they say there isn't any homework, but don't know how to overcome the homework inertia. And they may get tired of the constant battles about homework at night. Try to form an alliance with the school-teacher. Plan strategies together. After all, when your pre-teen gets into the middle high-school years, they will find it very helpful if they have developed a homework habit.

'Everyone hates me at school'

This is something to take seriously, although it is possible that tomorrow it will be quite different, and all will be well again. If a pre-teen feels that everyone hates them, there may be a problem with teasing or bullying, or it may be that they aren't very good at making friends. Everyone needs at least one good friend at school. Do they have someone to have lunch with, or do they go to the library by themselves? Do they join in games at recess and at lunchtime? Are they just no good at sport, and no-one picks them for their team? If you don't help them with social relationships at this age, they may go into their teenage years with damaged self-esteem, a poor reputation amongst their peers and a lot of misery associated with school.

'My teacher hates me'

This is most unlikely, although you can hardly expect teachers of pre-teens to like all the students in their class, in the same way you probably wouldn't like all the students (or their parents) yourself. Of course, a good teacher doesn't show preference, or demonstrate their personal likes and dislikes. It's worthwhile finding out why your child thinks that the teacher hates them. Do they misbehave in class, and get punished? Do they seem to pay no attention to the lessons, and disturb other students? Do they have a lot of difficulty with the work, and not try any more? Is the teacher a bit hard on them, in an effort to help them to apply themselves to their work? It's something to take up with the teacher yourself if your child can't solve the problem. Sometimes there is a genuine clash of personality which can't easily be resolved. Often, the teacher really would like to make things better for the child, but it takes more than good will to do this, and your child may have to make changes, too. One thing is certain: once a teenager is convinced that a teacher dislikes them, they usually stop working for them in class, and really give the teacher cause to dislike teaching them. So, it's good to resolve difficulties in relationships with teachers during the pre-teens.

When do you start talking about sex? When do they start thinking about it?

I recently gave a series of talks to a group of fourteen-year-old boys. They seemed pretty sophisticated for a group of teenagers, and had already had plenty of opportunities to learn about all aspects of human relationships in classwork at school and, one would have hoped, at home. I had given them the opportunity to write down questions anonymously and used these as a basis for discussion.

As I had expected, there were many questions about sex. What was remarkable was that despite a lot of knowledge and facts that these boys had been given, the anonymous questions expressed all the anxieties, doubts and uncertainties about their sexuality (and that of others) that young adolescents have probably always felt. Some were worried about their sexual feelings. Were they normal? Some were worried about their sexual development. Was it normal? Some still worried that masturbation could be harmful. Many were very unsure about how girls really felt about sex. When was the right age to start having sex? How would you know when you were ready?

You'd think that there has been so much said and written, and so many books and articles around, that everyone knows all about how to give children information about sex and introduce children to their sexuality. Sex education is given in most schools, and the topic of sex dominates so many videos, television shows and magazines. Yet children continue to learn most of what they think about sex from each other.

Sexuality is a new and private experience for every child

For every child, sexuality is a new and strange experience. It is exciting and can be scary: not so much because of lack of knowledge, but from the intense feelings that it stirs up at puberty. Sexuality has to be learnt in a child's own way. This occurs partly through asking questions at the right time, when they think about something, partly through experiencing things for themselves, and partly from talking to their friends, even though adults know so much more. Much of it is learnt in exciting ways that can't, and perhaps shouldn't, be shared fully with parents. Knowing the facts of reproduction helps, even the details about sexual behaviour and intercourse, but not as much as you might think. Every child wonders and questions and gets excited about so many things that adults may take for granted, or believe that the child would already know. Or perhaps shouldn't know. Or isn't ready to know.

Pre-teenage is the time for parents to be talking about sex

There's no doubt that sex is something that should be talked about well before the teenage years, and certainly in the pre-teens. Some parents still find it difficult to discuss the topic with their children. It's embarrassing for both parent and child. It certainly can be very awkward when they become teenagers. There are such strong taboos about sexual intimacy within families, that even talking about sex may seem to break the taboos and lead to discomfort all round, especially for the teenager. Parents may feel enlightened about their own sexuality, and want to share it with their children, but pre-teens and teenagers may actually be quite conservative in their own approach to sex. Teenagers can sometimes be quite critical of their parents' sex lives. This will set up further barriers to discussion about their own sexuality if parents leave it too late. Also, at their age, teenagers may already have had some exploration of sexual activity and have feelings of guilt or embarrassment they want to hide from parents.

Every child has to discover sex for themselves

Sexual feelings and behaviour are very personal at any age, especially for the pre-teen who is experiencing the excitement of awakening sexuality. It helps to have some knowledge about sex. It helps to know that sexual feelings happen to everyone, and that there is no shame in having them. It helps to be allowed to explore and experience sexuality at one's own pace. It helps to know that you can discuss things with a parent when you want to. But you have to discover it all for yourself, and you have to be allowed to do so.

This means that parents and teachers shouldn't be too intrusive about a pre-teen's sexuality. Some parents feel that children shouldn't have sexual feelings until they are more mature, and well into adolescence. Some children think that parents shouldn't have sexual feelings, and although they must have had sex to have had children, that should be quite enough. Children often think that sex is for young people, like teenagers and young adults. Not for parents and grandparents. It can be hard for parents and children to understand each other's views and perspective when the subject is brought up.

Pre-teens already have their own prejudices about sex

Throughout their early childhood, children absorb beliefs, attitudes and bits of information about sex. For instance, from an early age most children are reminded by their parents about the dangers of sexual abuse from strangers. Boys and girls are told not to talk to strange men, and not even to respond when someone smiles at them in the street. They are told not to trust strangers in case they have a sexual intention, even though statistics show that by far the most sexual abuse takes place within families or with a trusted friend or relative.

Boys are taught not to let anyone see or touch their genitals. This may be necessary to help children guard themselves from unscrupulous adults, but it invests strong feelings about the sexual organs, sexual behaviours and morality. A visit to the doctor becomes a nightmare if the doctor needs to examine the abdomen. Boys may enter their teen years with strong prejudices. Girls may distrust males. Boys may distrust adults. Both may be confused about their strong feelings and sexual urges.

If a child has had the misfortune to have been sexually abused, there is the risk that they will remain confused about their sexuality, even with expert counselling. They are likely to feel guilty to some extent, even though they have been reassured that it wasn't their fault. Sometimes a pre-teen may have enjoyed the sexual pleasure of an encounter with a sexually abusing adult or older child; then there is the additional guilt attached to the abuse. Sometimes a relative is accused of sexual abuse, perhaps a marriage breaks up or a relative goes before the law. The pre-teen cannot easily escape the feeling that they were to blame for what happened. It must colour their attitude towards sexual behaviour.

Most young children have had some sexual encounters between themselves. 'I'll show you mine if you show me yours.' 'Let's play doctors.' 'How big's yours?' All rather exciting for the child, and usually harmless. But what if they are caught, and their parents are disgusted or punish them? 'Don't you ever do that again. It's dirty.' 'I forbid you ever to play with that Mike again.' 'I'm ashamed of you.' The child gets to feel that sex is somehow dirty or shameful as a result of these experiences. When their sexual urges increase during puberty, the pre-teen or teenager may feel bad and confused about it.

How might parents and teachers make it more difficult for pre-teens to cope with their sexuality?

It's so easy to make mistakes about such a sensitive subject as sex, especially as each generation has its own views and experiences. Moral values and personal experience colour any discussion about sex. There are many pitfalls for parents and teachers in their approach to sexuality in a pre-teenager. Here are some of the ways that adults might make it more difficult for pre-teenagers to cope with their own feelings about their sexuality.

🖎 *By displaying strong attitudes about sex that go against their child's normal development.* They may do this by denying that a child has a strong interest, perhaps almost a preoccupation, with sex. Adults may show strong antagonism towards homosexual feelings at a stage when pre-teens will actually (and quite normally) feel attracted to, and prefer to play with, others of the same sex. It has been said that almost all pre-teenage boys are sexually excited by the sight of an erect penis — perhaps when they see a brother, friend or a pornographic video — but that doesn't mean that they are gay.

🖎 *By taking a vicarious interest in the sexual development and behaviour of their child.* It's a very personal thing. If they choose to tell you about their first pubic hair, or a girl's developing breast bud, or a boy's first ejaculation, that's fine, but it's up to them.

🖎 *By taking too strong a moral stance about sex that may be in conflict with the pre–teen and teenager's world.* It is, of course, important for parents to make it clear exactly where they stand about sexual behaviour. Family standards are very important. It can sometimes make it very difficult for the pre-teen if community expectations are very different. If this is the case, parents still have the duty of bringing up their child according to their own standards, but it may make it hard for their child if their moral stance is too strong and too binding. It might make it almost impossible for their child to discuss their own difficulties and problems with their parents.

- *By adopting a different attitude towards what is acceptable for boys, and what is expected for girls.* Some cultures do have a different standard for the sexes, but it can be very confusing for children in our society.

- *By focusing on 'safe sex'.* It is, of course, important that when teenagers and young adults start being sexually active, they avoid sexually transmitted diseases and unwanted pregnancy. But too much emphasis on this message implies that sexual activity is fine at their age, so long as a condom is worn. In their pre-teens very few children are ready for this kind of sexual activity; and those who do have sex may suffer more from the emotional confusion of the encounter than the physical risks.

- *By forgetting the strength of love.* Loving relationships can develop without the need for sexual intimacy. In discussing sex with a pre-teen, there is the danger that they might think that a loving relationship between people at any age has to lead to sex.

- *By giving too much knowledge and information too early, or when it isn't really wanted.* Discovering one's sexuality is a voyage of discovery, and although it helps to have a map and chart of dangerous waters, you don't need a tourist guide to go along with you. Especially your parents.

How can parents help?

- *By trying to avoid the above pitfalls!*
- *By talking about sex whenever the occasion seems right.* Perhaps after a television show when it comes up; always when they ask a question, particularly at bedtime when you aren't in a rush, and you plan to spend a few minutes with your children.
- *By not going into the matter in too much detail or for too long at first.* They might get confused, or worse still, bored! A short answer is excellent, and then wait for the next question.
- *By both fathers and mothers talking about sex with both daughters and sons.* But sometimes boys feel that they can discuss more intimate questions, like erections, with their father, and often girls feel more comfortable talking about things like menstruation with their mother. But there's no rule, whoever feels most comfortable about it is right.
- *By telling the pre–teen what to expect in their sexual development.* If they are late developers, they will have plenty of evidence of what is in store from their friends who have already started to develop. If they are entering puberty earlier than their friends, it may be quite worrying for them, although having an elder sibling of the same sex may help. Books with plenty of pictures aimed at the pre-teenager can help you in discussing puberty with them.

Drugs: what every parent should know

A group of pre-teenagers were talking together at lunchbreak at school. One of them said that her brother had made a bong.

'What does it look like?' they wanted to know. 'Where does he get the dope?' 'Will he let you try it?'

'He called it choofing. He said I'm too young. But I don't reckon I am.'

Anabel was boasting, but she was certainly curious about marijuana, and later the group talked about other drugs they had heard about, like ecstasy and acid and speed. They had some curious ideas about these drugs, but felt it was all very exciting. Most of the girls said that they would never try drugs. But one of the girls said that she had tried sniffing spray paint.

'It was great,' she said. 'You want to try it.'

Sooner or later every parent will be faced with the questions: What should my pre-teen or teenager know about drugs? Who should tell them about drugs, and at what age? If there is discussion, will it just encourage them to try them? Do parents really know what they are talking about if they have never tried drugs? Pre-teenagers might think that parents are just trying to scare them when there isn't really any danger if they are careful. Is marijuana really more dangerous than alcohol? Or is it safer?

The time to talk about drugs is when children show interest, and this is usually during their pre-teens. Parents need to be well informed about drugs if they are to give accurate information, and it is usually better to give facts than just opinion, and offer advice rather than make threats (although threats of dire punishment can be quite a powerful deterrent for pre-teenagers who basically want to be good).

It has been suggested that giving too much information about drugs to teenagers might actually encourage them to try for themselves. Whether this is true or not, it is less likely to lead to silly and dangerous experimentation if information is given by well-informed parents when their children are in their pre-teenage years. However, parents often are pretty ignorant themselves. Older brothers and sisters are likely to know more than their parents, but may or may not give accurate and sensible advice. 'You're too young' could be a come-on for some pre-teenagers. 'Don't talk about it, it's too stupid' might even stimulate interest. And then they might go to less appropriate sources for their information.

Illicit and so-called 'recreational' drugs have many dangers, but they also have effects that for some people are pleasant or exciting, or make them feel good. Otherwise, people wouldn't use them. If parents ignore discussing the pleasant effects, it might seem as if they don't really know as much as they say, or that they aren't giving correct information. That is not to say that parents should tell their pre-teenagers all about the potential pleasures of drug use and abuse, but they should at least know the facts.

Marijuana

Its many street names including dope, weed, hash, pot, grass and THC (which is short for its chemical name — tetrahydrocannabinol). Some varieties are much stronger than others. Some, for example skunk, have been fortified to give a more powerful drug effect.

Marijuana and the related and more powerful drugs, hash and hash oil, come from the cannabis plant. There are several varieties of cannabis with differing concentrations of the active drug, but many preparations of marijuana have a much higher concentration of the drug than the leaf of *Cannabis sativa* that is commonly and, in most states, illegally grown in many back yards and houses in Australia. Marijuana is the dried leaf. Hashish is the resin that comes from the plant.

Marijuana actually contains several potent drugs that affect the human mind. The main one is called THC. Hash and hash oil have far higher concentrations of the drug than the leaf of the plant, and are often added to the leaf or to tobacco to give a much greater drug effect.

Marijuana is absorbed into the body very quickly, reaching the brain in a few seconds. This leads to a 'high' that reaches a peak in about 20 minutes and lasts about 2 or 3 hours. The drug remains in the body for much longer, and the harmful effects remain for many hours after the feeling of pleasure has gone.

The 'high' of marijuana (being stoned or smashed) is one of sedation and tranquillity, sometimes with a mild hallucination. The muscles relax, and things don't seem to matter so much. Perception of time and space may alter, and there is often a delay between putting thought into action. Many users find that they get very hungry. They get red eyes (which they learn to disguise with eye drops or dark glasses).

Many teenagers say that even if they are stoned, they can snap out of it if they really need to. Perhaps they can lose the peaceful sedation feeling quickly, but the adverse effects on their brain linger for hours after the pleasure has gone.

The possible harmful effects are largely on the brain; although the drug is quickly absorbed into many other body organs including the liver, the reproductive organs and the lungs. Chronic marijuana smokers may have an even greater risk for cancer than cigarette smokers. In the pre-teenage years, heavy use may have impaired their growth and caused a delay in their puberty development. The effects on the brain, however, are the most immediately worrying. There is a lag time between thought and action, which makes it dangerous to do some things that require skill and quick reflexes like driving or handling machinery. There can be loss of efficiency in doing some tasks that need planning and coordination. There may be short-term memory loss, which interferes with learning and study.

Heavy use of the drug can lead to paranoid thoughts and panic attacks, and people may have an altered perception of their body: a limb may seem very large or out of proportion. Most worrying of all, though very uncommon, is the development of a psychotic mental illness such as schizophrenia brought on by marijuana.

Occasional use of marijuana may not have a permanent effect, but chronic use probably does. This is known from observing heavy users, and also from research studies done on monkey brains. The most worrying effects on teenagers who use marijuana regularly include loss of motivation, learning difficulties and memory deficits that seem to be long standing (if not permanent) in many cases.

It has been suggested that addiction doesn't occur with marijuana. Certainly people can become dependent on the drug, and I have known many older teenagers who have been heavy users for years and find themselves unable to give it up. When they do try, they may become distressed and can't sleep. On the other hand, coming off this drug may be far less painful than other drugs that are known to be highly addictive, such as tobacco and the narcotics; and there is no doubt that even very heavy users can give up quite quickly if they really want to, and if they receive the help they need.

Inhalants

There are many volatile substances that pre-teens and teenagers may use to inhale or sniff to give them a very quick high. These include glues, dry-cleaning fluid, spray paints (especially the metallic ones), petrol and very many other substances. Teenagers who inhale metallic chrome-based aerosols call it 'chroming'. Children may sniff them directly from the container, from soaked tissues and cloths or from plastic bags. Different materials may have different effects, but in general they give a feeling of relaxation, sleepiness and wellbeing. There may be a relaxation of social inhibitions, and some inhalants can give hallucinatory experiences. Sometimes users seem to be drunk and confused. One teenager I knew called the inhalants the 'dream drugs'.

There are a number of bad effects from inhaling volatile substances. They can affect learning and memory. They can damage the liver. They can lead to death.

LSD 'acid'

LSD (lysergic acid diethylamide) is a synthetic drug and comes in the form of droplets which are often absorbed on small squares of paper, called 'tabs'. LSD causes hallucinations of both vision and sound. It is said to 'expand the consciousness', giving an altered perception of the world with vivid colours and magnified shapes and sounds. LSD is relatively cheap and very easy to hide, so it can be very hard to prevent its use.

Some people using acid experience 'bad trips' with panic that sometimes amounts to terror. This can happen to people who have previously had only 'good trips', and there can be 'flashbacks' with recurrence of the symptoms long after the actual bad trip. Like other hallucinogenic drugs, including marijuana, LSD has been known to bring on serious mental illness.

Some of the other side effects include dizziness, weakness and nausea. There may be dilatation of the pupils of the eye and high blood pressure. The immediate effects of LSD start to wear off within about 12 hours.

Amphetamines 'speed'

Amphetamines, in the form of dexamphetamine, have been around for many years, being used in tablet form to control weight. Speed can be taken as tablets, or injected into a vein. It provides a high rather like cocaine, with a strong feeling of wellbeing and euphoria. Fatigue disappears and there is a feeling of physical strength and mental ability. This soon wears off, leaving irritability and fatigue. Injecting into a vein has all the dangers of contaminated materials with the drug and infection of the hepatitis and the HIV viruses from shared needles.

Ecstasy

Ecstasy (methylenedioxymethamphetamine) is a hallucinogen, like LSD. It is made synthetically and is becoming readily available, being used mainly by young adults and older teenagers. The strength of the drug can vary, and it can be particularly harmful when mixed with other drugs at teenage parties. Harmful effects may include irrational behaviour, depression and vomiting. Whether there are long-term harmful effects is not known yet, although there have been several deaths from taking ecstasy. No matter what teenagers and pre-teenagers are told by their friends (and older people) who are encouraging them to try drugs, there is always a danger, and this danger cannot always be predicted.

Household and prescription drugs

Most parents keep medications in the home. Most homes have painkillers in a cupboard or cabinet somewhere: perhaps they are left over from some illness when not all the medication was used or perhaps someone in the house has needed sedatives or tranquillisers at some time. Pre-teens and teenagers have no trouble in finding these, and may use them as a 'cocktail' to add to alcohol or mix them with each other just to try the effect. The greatest danger is a possible (or perhaps deliberate) overdose, and many suicide attempts have used household drugs, such as Panadol, that have come from the home cabinet. But even trying out a drug from the medicine chest or bathroom cupboard for fun can lead to serious consequences.

Health and nutrition

Getting eating habits in good shape before things can go wrong

'She's got very thin, doctor. I knew she was trying to eat healthy foods and cut down on snacks, but I hadn't realised how much weight she had lost until I saw her in a T-shirt last week.'

Lisa's mother was worried that her daughter was dieting and perhaps this had got out of hand.

'I'm not dieting,' said Lisa. 'I'm just eating healthy foods. What's wrong with that?'

Lisa's father said that there was probably something wrong with her, and she should see the family doctor. He hadn't really noticed how little she ate because the family seldom ate their meals together. 'What with all the homework they have to do, and the TV shows they can't miss, we tend to eat by ourselves in front of the TV. They help themselves and just make their own breakfast and lunches.'

Lisa was just thirteen and had only recently reached puberty. She was not eating enough at main meals and had few snacks or milk drinks. What was surprising was that her family hadn't really noticed this until she had lost a lot of weight and was quite thin. Perhaps it wasn't so surprising, as the family didn't often eat together, and Lisa was clearly disguising her thin body from her parents by wearing floppy sweaters.

When children are small their parents usually decide what and how much they should eat and drink. As they grow older, their appetite and personal likes and dislikes of certain foods have greater influence, and this gradually determines what and how much they eat. Sometimes parents let their children decide how much to help themselves from the family meals or snacks. Maybe they worry if they think their child is growing too slowly, or getting too thin, or seems pale or tired, and wonder if it's due to something missing from their diet. But they know that nature has a general rule that almost always works: if there is plenty of food around, a healthy child won't be under-nourished. A child's natural instinct determines this, even though the actual amounts of food needed by different children may be very different.

Unfortunately, in our society this rule doesn't always work out during their teens. Social pressures, worry about the shape of their body, diet fads and the availability of very attractive fast foods and drinks may override the natural instincts for good nutrition. Sometimes pre-teens and teenagers get inappropriate advice from nutrition experts. For all of these reasons, parents still have an important role in making sure their children have enough of the good foods throughout childhood and adolescence. This is especially important in early puberty and during adolescence when the growth rate increases, and teenage social life begins to intrude into family life.

It's very hard to change eating behaviour once a child becomes an adolescent. They can get into very entrenched habits. They may defy their parents, and when it comes to eating, parents are almost powerless against a stubborn determined teenager.

Healthy eating habits that are established during the pre-teens will help during their teens

The time to make sure children have good habits is in their pre-teens, and the place to do it is at the family dinner-table. The people to do it are the parents (with the help of the rest of the family).

Be aware of the things that tend to sabotage good eating habits in the pre-teenager. These include TV and sports training, as well as getting up late and missing breakfast in the rush for school. Family members who are always late for meals at night may make it hard for a pre-teenager to maintain a good routine. Bad tempered teenage brothers or sisters who argue around the table can be a pain. But the worst of all are the social and media pressures to have a slim body.

There are several positive steps that parents might take if they are concerned that their pre-teenager is in danger of getting into bad eating habits.

TRY TO MAKE SURE THAT AT LEAST ONE MEAL A DAY IS A FAMILY MEAL

Ideally, this is the evening meal where everyone sits down together, so that it is also a social occasion. It may be increasingly hard to do this as children grow up and sports training, part-time jobs and social pressures all compete with family routine. If it is impossible to do this every night, have rules that it should happen at least several times a week, with priority over almost everything else.

DISCOURAGE TAKING PLATES OF FOOD TO EAT IN FRONT OF THE TV

Even when everyone wants to see the same show, watching TV is a very isolating activity: no-one is allowed to talk (except during the ads, and even then some people are captivated by the commercials). Mothers don't really notice what their children are eating, fathers don't have the chance to get to know their children and what they have been doing. And if an eating disorder does develop during teenage years (which, unfortunately, is not uncommon), it will be essential to go back to family meals away from the TV.

TRY TO MAKE SURE EVERYONE HAS SOME BREAKFAST

This sets the stage for a healthy and productive day. It is often the time to have some fruit juice, cereal and milk: all providing essential foods. People (especially teenagers) who skip breakfast tend to snack more during the day, often on less healthy foods, and they eat to excess. People who skip meals to keep their weight down often fast during the early part of the day, and then binge later. They get angry with themselves, and they become determined to skip breakfast the next day to make up for it. This makes for a vicious cycle of skipping meals and then bingeing, and can lead to bulimia (binge eating followed by vomiting) later in adolescence. This is a rather common and worrying eating disorder, mainly experienced by young women.

TRY NOT TO HAVE FOOD AND EATING A FOCUS OF ARGUMENTS

If you feel that your pre-teen isn't eating sensibly, be firm. Put on the plate the food *you* think they should have (not what they say they want), and leave it at that, trying to avoid pressures and comments. The discussion at mealtime should be around more pleasant topics and family affairs.

DISCOURAGE YOUR PRE-TEENAGERS AND TEENAGERS FROM GOING ON A DIET

Diets mean to a pre-teenager eating less of the foods they like so as to lose weight. They don't work and they may do harm. Sensible eating and plenty of exercise are much more likely to be effective.

(See page 117 for a discussion on sensible eating and exercise.)

If, despite all this, you feel that your pre-teenager is focusing too much on diets and on losing weight, and you worry that they may develop anorexia or another eating disorder, get help early rather than putting it off too long. Eating disorders aren't too difficult to correct in the early teens when they haven't become entrenched. The longer they have been present, the harder they are to treat.

Lisa was rather underweight, and had stopped growing. This was not unexpected, as children who don't put on weight, particularly if they lose weight for any reason, put their growth at risk. It had all started when she decided that she wanted to be a ballet dancer, but felt she had no hope because she wasn't skinny enough.

Lisa had a few tests to rule out a physical cause for being underweight, but these proved normal. At this stage we didn't identify any serious underlying emotional disorder in Lisa, and changing the family focus on meals and social behaviour was the first step in helping her. Her mother took over the family meals and helped everyone to their food at the table. TV was banned at meal times (despite quite a few protests) but the family started to talk to each other, which was a bonus for everyone. And Lisa started to put on a bit of weight.

Puppy fat: or is it?

Jessica had been a rather large girl from early childhood. She had been a 'perfect' baby, gaining weight very well in infancy; in fact, she was well rounded as a toddler and quite big when she went to kindergarten. Her mother said that she hadn't been worried because she was one of the taller children there, and felt that she could 'carry her weight' it wouldn't be a problem.

Jessica was eleven now, and in grade 6 at primary school. The trouble was that in the last 6 months she seemed to be putting on more and more weight, and was getting teased by one of the boys in her class. Her father said that it was just puppy fat, and she would grow out of it. Some relatives said that she should go on a diet. Her grandmother wasn't so sure, because she had always had a weight problem, and hadn't found diets much help for Jessica's mother when she had been a child.

'She's started puberty,' her mother said. 'I can't stop her eating. Could it be her hormones?'

Jessica's mother's concern was quite reasonable. Children are often teased when they are overweight, and she was worried that this teasing might get worse when Jessica went to high school. But could she really do anything about it?

Most pre-teen obesity has a genetic cause

The most common cause for pre-teenagers and teenagers to be fat is genetic. We inherit our body figure, just as we tend to inherit our height. This has been shown in studies of identical and nonidentical twins. Identical twins tend to have the same body figure and the same degree of fatness as each other. Nonidentical twins often have very different figures, even though they have been brought up the same way. Another study, in Scandinavia, showed that children adopted at birth grew up to have figures like their biological parents rather than like their adoptive parents. Things can affect this inherited tendency, such as illness, emotional problems and a very sedentary lifestyle. Very rarely, a hormonal imbalance can be found as the cause.

Puberty usually starts in the pre-teens, and in girls puberty makes weight control much more difficult. At this time, the hormone oestrogen, which is so important in turning a girl into a woman, also influences the amount and distribution of fat in the body. This is really a natural part of puberty, and gives a young woman the rounded appearance that was (and still is) so much admired by young men. But these days most girls hate it, and they are very influenced by thin models, the advertising media, fashionable clothes and the entertainment industry. There are many other reasons why so many girls want to be thin, none of which are very helpful in making a girl on the brink of adolescence feel good about her body if she is a bit overweight.

Could it be due to a medical or glandular cause?

It is, of course, worthwhile checking if there is a medical cause for a pre-teen to be overweight. In general, if a child is of average height and growing normally, being fat is not due to a glandular cause, because the hormonal imbalance that can make people fat also stops children from growing.

Sometimes a drawn-out illness that has made a child very inactive, but didn't reduce their appetite, will lead to excessive weight gain. Sometimes an emotional illness can lead to such over-eating that a pre-teenager becomes very overweight. This usually develops quite rapidly, and it's obvious to everyone that they are eating compulsively, and it's not just because they are hungry.

It is worth having a medical check with your doctor for overweight if:

- your child is shorter than you would expect for family height
- your child is not growing as expected
- the weight gain is recent or excessive, and you can't find a reason
- your child seems to have an emotional problem associated with putting on weight
- there are other symptoms such as headaches as well as the weight gain
- You are worried! That's always a perfectly good reason for a medical checkup.

And if there doesn't seem to be a physical cause for the excess weight?

This is the usual situation, and it can be very frustrating for everyone, including the pre-teenager, particularly if people blame them for their weight gain. They may try hard to cut down eating, but still not lose much weight. Names hurt, too: 'fat slob', 'fatso' and 'greedyguts' are very unfair and unkind.

It's worse if people assume that the pre-teen is fat because they are greedy or overeat all the time, and it's probably untrue anyway. You have only to look at what some very slim boys eat to realise that most fat children don't really eat more than other children. Some have been shown to eat less, in fact; but of course some overweight children do eat a lot more than they need, particularly if they are bored or spend much of their time watching television.

It is usually best to focus on physical activity, on having fun with friends, on feeling good

Many overweight children are just as active as other children, but some studies have suggested that, on average, fat children spend more time watching television than slim children; and that the more hours a week children spend in front of the TV set, the fatter they may become. Not all reports agree with these studies; but everyone agrees that it's good for children to be physically active. This is especially important for pre-teens, because habits of exercise (or lack of exercise) learnt at this age tend to carry over into adolescence and adult life.

Exercise is good for all of us and at all ages. It is especially important for growing children, and pre-teens as they embark on puberty. But some children don't like much physical activity. Some just naturally prefer playing quietly or doing art and indoor hobbies; they only go outside if they are pushed out and the doors are locked, or if friends come round and want to play outside. Computer games, videos and television have been a great trap for these children.

It isn't always helpful, or even practical, to tell a child to go outside and play, especially if they are on their own. Pre-teens need to have fun with physical activities, and they need to do them with someone else. Parents who buy exercise bikes and walking machines for their overweight pre-teen usually watch the equipment gathering dust and cobwebs from lack of use after the first few weeks. Trampolines are better because they are more fun for your child, and there's usually someone else to share the fun. Bike riding is very good, provided there's someone to ride with. As a pre-teen, walking by yourself is very boring, and you look stupid if you aren't going anywhere in particular. Dogs are good company on a walk. So are parents (and it's good for them, too). Parents can have very good conversations with their pre-teen on walks, and it's a marvellous way to really learn what they are interested in and what worries them. But do it now, before they become teenagers, or they might not think it cool to walk around with a parent where they might be seen by their friends.

Some overweight pre-teens enjoy group activities, such as jazz ballet or aerobics. Some will be happy to join a club for netball, tennis or another sport. Some will get a lot from joining a youth club or scouts.

- All these things will have at least four potential gains:
- they lead to more activity that burns up calories
- they get them out of the house and away from the TV set for a while
- they will feel better, more confident and less bored
- they might make new friends

What about diets?

Diets for pre-teens seldom help in the long run. They may benefit from looking at some of their eating habits, and cut down on snacks and other foods that have a lot of kilojoules (calories). The main food type to look at is the fat content, and sometimes quite a lot of kilojoules can be saved by reducing full-cream dairy products and thick sandwich spreads. Fried foods, just the things pre-teens usually like best, may need to be restricted. Some children get a lot of kilojoules from drinks. Soft drinks, except the low kilojoule ones, usually contain about 10% sugar, and even pure orange juice has this amount of naturally occurring fruit sugar.

If it seems that your pre-teen is having rather a lot of these so-called 'energy dense' foods, and you have difficulty in working out how much is enough, it would be very helpful to discuss it with a dietitian. A dietitian will often have good ideas for alternative foods with less energy value, and could reassure you that your pre-teenager is having adequate nutrition. Don't forget that in cutting down on your pre-teenager's favourite foods, you may be depriving them of one of their main pleasures in life.

Do overweight children have low self-esteem?

It may seem surprising, but most overweight children, including pre-teens, have quite good self-esteem. They may not feel so good about their figure, but are quite sure of themselves in other ways. Some overweight pre-teenagers, however, do have rather poor self-esteem, particularly if they have found it hard to cope with teasing at school. This could be an important factor in making it difficult for them to change their lifestyle. They may think 'What's the point? I'm no good anyway'. These children need a lot of support and encouragement, and the chance to succeed in something they do. All the more reason why they should join in group activities and clubs.

Don't expect too much

It will be important for pre-teens who are overweight, and who have inherited their figure, not to have too high an expectation about losing weight. They possibly won't lose much after the first few enthusiastic weeks, and when the weight goes back on, there is a risk that they may feel a failure, or that they are letting you down. We must be very careful not to set such a child up for failure. It may be better to measure success by increased amounts of activity, or sport, or social gains, or happiness, rather than a weight change.

We didn't put Jessica on a diet, though there were some suggestions for changes in her snacks that seemed sensible. She still had treats now and again. She did, however, ride her bike for half an hour most days with her elder sister, and sometimes she and her mother and the dog would go for long walks together. She didn't lose a lot of weight, though she certainly didn't continue to put it on. Her grandmother bought her some new clothes, and everyone thought she looked great. The boy who used to tease her eventually got bored by it all and stopped.

Food, diets, myths and fads

I remember some years ago a mother brought her twelve-year-old son to see me because he had a terrible diet. His general practitioner had been sufficiently concerned that he arranged a blood count to make sure the boy wasn't anaemic, and checked on the calcium in his blood and his cholesterol level. Everything was quite normal. But the

GP was concerned that the strange food preferences would be interfering with his growth and health.

Sam, his mother told me, lived solely on chocolate flavoured milk, which he had for breakfast, lunch, and tea. He didn't like fruit. If he was to eat any meat, it would be hamburgers and maybe sausages. Vegetables? You'd have to be joking. He would touch none of the wretched things, no matter how his mother cooked them. 'It's not as if we don't have good meals at our house. All the rest of the family eat healthy foods. I have tried everything to make him eat good foods. His father's given up growling at him.'

The odd thing was that Sam seemed perfectly healthy, and he was growing well. He was well nourished, and he thought all the fuss was a bit stupid. He was rather insulted when I asked him if he got constipated (too much milk and too little fibre can have this effect), but his mother said that judging by the hours he spent on the loo, he probably was. And he did get occasional stomach pains.

Actually, Sam did have a reasonable amount of the essential foods he needed. He did like potato, which gave him his vitamin C, and he also had some orange juice. Milk gave him plenty of the vitamin B group and protein and energy. He would probably need more iron in his diet when he entered the growing phase of puberty, but he seemed to be getting enough from his hamburgers at the moment.

It just shows how children can sometimes be healthy despite strange food habits. But not everyone; and not when they get into puberty, when rapid growth and development, and the increased activity of the teenage years, make many demands on nutrition.

Traditionally, mothers have known what to feed their children on and how much. They learnt this from their own experience and from their own mothers. In a society where a wide variety of foods are affordable and in abundance, it is hard to become malnourished in childhood, and not really much excuse at any age, unless there are strong emotional or cultural constraints on food. Almost everyone has strong views about food (it has to be organic, natural, healthy, low-fat, high-fibre, free of preservatives and colouring, sugar free, low salt, starch free ...), and the newspapers and magazines are full of advice. The trouble is that diets have become so popular, and there seem to be so many experts about, you might think that parents should be undertaking special studies on nutrition if they are to bring up their children safely.

What are the barriers to healthy eating in the pre-teen years?

It is a mistake to apply theories about heart disease in middle-aged people to growing children. Experts who advocate low-fat, low-cholesterol diets for everyone are focusing on the needs of a different age group with a set of problems that are not applicable to growing children. But they sometimes scare parents and teenagers into thinking that they are not eating healthy foods if they have anything with any fat or any sugar in them. Teachers sometimes incorporate these views in school when teaching about healthy living.

It is unwise to listen to all the theories about harmful foods. Some so-called 'experts' believe that all illness in childhood is due to dairy products in foods, or yeasts, or preservatives, or wheat products. Now it is true that about 1% of children can't easily tolerate milk products due to a milk allergy. In some Asian countries people do not have the enzymes in the bowel needed to digest milk sugars. For them, too much milk or dairy products after early infancy may cause trouble in their digestion. But in Australia most children thrive on milk, cheese, yoghurt and other milk products, and get most of their calcium from these foods.

It is also true that those few children who have coeliac disease can't tolerate wheat products. But everyone else can. It is also true that a very few children seem to get hyped up on certain food-colouring agents, especially red colourings which may occur in cordials and some sweets and jellies. Obviously, it's good if those children avoid these foods (though it's very hard to do so, as it excludes a lot of soft drinks and sweets that children and teenagers like so much).

Although some people have been convinced that sugar is bad for children, there is virtually no evidence to support this. It is impossible anyway to avoid all sugars, as they occur in many foods like fruit and milk. There was a time when some people thought that bad behaviour was due to hypoglycaemia, or low levels of sugar in the blood. Although hypoglycaemia can affect a very few people in the community, it is very rare in children (apart from those with diabetes having insulin) and there is no scientific evidence that sugar is harmful as part of a growing child's nutrition. It does *not* cause diabetes.

Salt is another popular culprit and is of interest because it is associated with high blood pressure in adults, particularly those with a family history of high blood pressure. It is now realised that some people can't tolerate a high salt intake, and for them it can lead to high blood pressure. This does not appear to be a problem until well into adolescence or adult life, and children and pre-teens (and most teenagers) seem to be unharmed by the high salt content of many fast foods and savoury snacks. It is true that most people do have more salt than they really need, so perhaps it is wise for pre-teens to get used to avoiding too much salt on their food or using too much in cooking. If they are one of those who would be affected by too much salt, they may avoid high blood pressure in later life, and they won't have the taste for salty foods that could be harmful.

What about minerals and vitamins? Most pre-teens will be having plenty of all the necessary vitamins and minerals from the family meals and snacks that their parents give them. It is seldom necessary to give extra vitamins or minerals unless a child is on a very odd diet that excludes a range of foods.

Although everyone needs vitamins and minerals, and although deficiencies in the diet can cause serious ill health and disease, there is no evidence that giving children more than they need makes them any healthier. Why waste money on capsules and vitamin supplements if they are getting plenty in good food?

An exception is iron in girls as they enter puberty. Many girls will be getting barely enough iron, and when they start to menstruate they may suffer from a lack of iron to replace that lost in their periods. If this deficiency becomes severe, they may become anaemic. Although many foods have iron, meat is the richest source, and if a child is having meat several times a week, parents don't need to worry about iron deficiency.

What about diets?

Except for those children who have been diagnosed by a reputable specialist as having a genuine food intolerance, or a condition like diabetes, there is one very good piece of advice about any dieting for pre-teen: **Don't let your pre-teen go on a diet.** But since so many magazines say you should, why not?

Firstly, pre-teens don't need diets, even though they may benefit from sensible eating plans.

Secondly, diets are likely to lead to food fads, which can only cause harm.

Thirdly, dieting might get out of hand and lead to an eating disorder like anorexia nervosa.

Fourthly, diets often fail to do whatever they set out to do (such as lose weight or improve behaviour), and this causes disappointment and recriminations.

Fifthly, few pre-teens can stick to a diet no matter how hard they try, so they fail and then feel guilty and might get blamed for breaking their diet and putting on weight.

What about sensible eating plans?

This does make sense, because most people are really interested in food and nutrition, and want the best for their children. Eating plans don't mean having a diet, but they do mean having some general principles for good nutrition that families can follow. Most families do this naturally, but some can benefit from having a plan, especially when both parents are working and mealtimes and food preparation are a rush and a chore. It can also be helpful if your pre-teen decides they want to go on a diet, then you can at least say they can follow a sensible eating plan. It can be reassuring to know that children, especially pre-teens, are developing healthy eating habits which will be a basis for good health in their teenage years.

Here are some broad principles for sensible eating.

HAVE THREE MEALS A DAY

Don't miss breakfast. Even though everyone is in a rush for work and school at breakfast time, it is very unwise to skip this meal. Children focus on schoolwork better if they have eaten breakfast. It can be an enjoyable time for the family to start the day. If a pre-teen is worried about their weight, skipping breakfast seems to make weight control much harder, probably because it leads to over-snacking later in the day. Breakfast is a meal where many children get their vitamin C from juice, their calcium from milk and their fibre from breakfast cereal and toast.

TRY TO HAVE THE FAMILY MEAL TOGETHER IN THE EVENING

It is often the only social occasion for all the family to meet together. It is often the meal that contains good foods like vegetables, meat, potato or pasta. Parents can be assured that everyone is getting plenty. Even if it is very difficult to arrange this, because of sport commitments, or father is home late from work or younger children are too tired to wait for the older children, try at least to do so two or three times a week.

HAVE A VARIETY OF HEALTHY FOODS THAT THE PRE-TEEN LIKES AVAILABLE FOR AFTER-SCHOOL SNACKING

Teenagers get almost a third of their daily food intake from snacks, so it's a good idea for pre-teens to get into the habit of thinking of some healthy foods after school. It's a good time for fruit, yoghurt, dry biscuits and cheese, toast and vegemite, or perhaps hot soups in winter.

INTRODUCE NEW FOODS FROM TIME TO TIME AT FAMILY MEALS
You may be surprised that your pre-teenager finds they like some
of the foods they wouldn't touch a few years earlier, like pumpkin,
broccoli or even fish. Teenagers can be rather conservative in
their food tastes; get them to try things out while they are
prepared to do so.

*DON'T FORGET THAT RAW VEGETABLES ARE JUST AS GOOD FOR
YOUR HEALTH, AND OFTEN BETTER THAN COOKED VEGETABLES*
Pre-teens often like salads, and can get all the vitamin C and other
good things that they need from vegetables.

DISCOURAGE FAD DIETS
Sometimes pre-teen girls decide to lose weight by avoiding foods
that they have been told are fattening. As these often include meat,
chicken and dairy foods, they may be missing out on important
minerals and protein. Many teenage girls who have become
severely anorexic have started off with a diet of 'healthy eating' at
this time. It may seem healthy, and it may comply with the National
Heart Foundation's advice for overweight middle-aged people, and
it may be sensible for weight control for adults who are getting fat,
but it is seldom a good idea for pre-teens, who are just embarking
on puberty. Puberty is the time for the development of the mature
body, so there is an increased need for energy foods and protein.
Puberty is the time when the bones broaden and strengthen. Forty
per cent of the body's skeleton development, including
strengthening of bones with calcium, occurs in adolescence. So
puberty is not the time to start fad diets.

*DON'T HAVE TOO MANY ARGUMENTS ABOUT FOOD AT THE
DINNER TABLE*
If you think that your pre-teenager isn't eating properly (either
too much or too little) or is avoiding the most healthy foods, be
firm at the table but reserve discussion until later.

TRY TO HAVE YOUR PRE-TEEN EAT THREE DAIRY FOODS EACH DAY
This might be in the form of milk, cheese, yoghurt or ice cream.
They will need the calcium from these foods.

TRY TO HAVE FOODS WITH PLENTY OF IRON
Prepare iron-rich foods, such as red meat, two or three times a week.

TRUST YOUR OWN JUDGMENT
Parents usually do know best when it comes to feeding their
children.

School and learning difficulties

Reading difficulties

'He's never been exactly keen on school, but since he started high school this year he is getting bad reports and even though we try to supervise him, he doesn't do any homework. He says he doesn't get any to do; but when I went to the parent–teacher night they said that there was homework, but he never handed it in.'

Twelve-year-old Julian said that he hated school and couldn't be bothered with homework. He only went to school because he had to, and to see his friends. The main problem, however, was that reading was a real burden for him. He hated it because he found it difficult, and even when he had managed to struggle through a page of a book, he had put so much effort into the process of reading that he hadn't understood or remembered any of it. So what was the point of trying? What took other students a few minutes to read, took him hours. Even then, he didn't really understand what he had read because he hadn't remembered it.

His mother said he could write, but his spelling was so bad that no-one could make sense of half of what he had written. Even he couldn't make much of what he had written with so much difficulty. So why bother?

Some children learn to read quite easily, many even before they start school. They learn by watching the books that their parents read to them in bed at night, and they want to know what the letters say and the words mean. Most children learn without trouble in the early primary school years and get enormous pleasure in reading books to their teachers and parents. It is a great sense of achievement for them. It is also a great reassurance for their parents, because they know that success in education depends on the ability to read rapidly and easily. This is just as true in the age of television and electronic information as it always was.

For some children, however, this process of learning to read doesn't come easily. For a few it doesn't come at all in primary school. For many of these children, the full effect of not being able to read easily isn't felt until they are at secondary school, and by then it may be getting too late. School will be boring and a burden (except perhaps for art, woodwork, PE and other subjects that don't require so much reading). Homework won't get done. Assignments won't get handed in. Reports might get worse and worse, and perhaps the student, now in their teenage years and with all the extra priorities and distractions of adolescence, will just give up on learning at school.

How could reading difficulties get missed in early primary school?

Perhaps the child has got by in primary school without having to read, because he was quite bright, has been a good talker and class participant and his parents have 'helped' him with homework by reading to him and helping with his writing and spelling. Perhaps they have known all along that he was having difficulties but hoped he would improve with time.

Sometimes children who are very well behaved in class, and sit quietly without causing bother to the teacher, aren't noticed as much as the children who cause trouble. This may be another reason why some children who can't read easily may get to their pre-teens without coming to the attention of the school. Whatever the reason, if the problem isn't sorted out before they get into secondary school they will have great difficulties there.

Sometimes reading difficulty is just part of a general learning problem

Some children have general learning difficulties, perhaps as the result of mild intellectual disability, and reading may be just one learning task amongst many that is too difficult. Parents and teachers usually recognise these children quite early in primary school because they are struggling in all aspects of learning. Occasionally, if they don't cause trouble in class and their difficulty is only mild, their disability may not be picked up at school until they are in their pre-teens or even later, which is a great pity because they clearly need special help. Parents usually know if their child is struggling with schoolwork.

Why do some children, who are otherwise bright, have so much difficulty in reading?

There can be several reasons why children can't read easily, and it's usually helpful to try to sort them out so that appropriate help can be given. Here are some of the reasons why a child can't read even though they seem to be quite bright in other ways.

MISSING OUT AT A CRITICAL TIME IN PRIMARY SCHOOL WHEN OTHER CHILDREN ARE LEARNING TO READ
This could happen if the child has been ill, and missed a lot of school; or if the family has had to make a number of moves, and the child has had several changes of school and hasn't had a chance to settle in. It could also happen if the child had hearing problems from ear infections at that time, so they had difficulty in understanding what was said in class when they were being taught to read.

There are critical times during a child's development when they are most receptive to learning to read; in the same way that children's development at certain ages enables them to learn to walk, talk or use a spoon to feed themselves. Most children are ready to learn to read at about the age of five, when they are starting primary school. Some are ready earlier, some a bit later. If they miss out then, they could be in trouble.

Slow development of the part of the brain responsible for reading

The ability to read actually depends on a series of steps that are needed in order to read fluently and easily. For instance, the brain has first to see the letters and words. It then has to interpret them into intelligible words to understand them. Even then a reader has to remember what they have just read so that they can make some sense of sentences, and put it in sequence with everything else that they are reading.

This can be just as difficult a task for some children as it would be for us to make sense of, say, the complex characters in Chinese writing or Arabic letters if we have never learnt that language.

So there are several steps in the process of reading that might go wrong in the development of the child's brain and lead to difficulty in learning to read. This can happen even when the rest of the brain is able to work perfectly efficiently. The child could be quite intelligent, and be able to function quite well except for this one thing: the ability to read fluently and with understanding.

We have known about this problem for a long time, and know that it can affect many children, perhaps as many as one in every hundred. It has been sometimes called a 'specific learning disability', and sometimes referred to as 'dyslexia'. This word just means difficulty in reading. The terms are just labels. However, it does help to know that it isn't due to laziness, stupidity or bad teaching.

There are a number of tests that a child can be given to check if there is a specific learning disability. Some are given by educational psychologists or neuropsychologists. Others can be given by educational experts or a specialist paediatrician.

PROBLEMS WITH VISION

A child may have difficulty in reading if they have a visual difficulty. Apart from general visual disturbance, which is usually very obvious by the pre-teens, the child might have difficulty in seeing clearly at close range, even though their distance vision might be quite adequate. Some optometrists and eye specialists believe that some children have difficulty in focusing, or in getting both eyes exactly fixed on the same spot. In that case, they are often seen to be squinting at the print, or holding their eyes very close to the page.

The child might say that the print seems to be jumping about when they try to focus on it; or the child gets very tired looking at print for a long time, as their eyes have to strain to keep the print in focus.

If parents notice any of these things, they should get their child's vision tested.

INAPPROPRIATE TEACHING METHODS

Some children are lucky. They find it so easy to learn to read when they are young that they practically teach themselves, even before they get to school. Others are unlucky because they do not find it so easy, and may need expert teaching. These children suffer if the teaching they get at primary school is not appropriate because they rely so much on the way they are taught at school.

Unfortunately there was a period in recent years when teachers thought that the best way to teach children to read was the 'whole word' method. In this method, children were taught to recognise words by their general shape, and not sound them out. This is certainly a skill that comes with practice for most people, and that is the way most adults do read. But it has been discredited as a teaching method in many countries and shown to be a bad way for children to learn to read, and a disaster for those children who have real difficulties in reading. The traditional method of sounding out letters and recognising the sounds that groups of letters make, called the 'phonics' method, has been shown to be the best way. However, there are many children who have been taught the whole word method (look and see), and have never been able to read with ease or pleasure: They were not well taught at primary school, and the result is a lasting disability that will become more and more a handicap as they enter their secondary-school years.

What can parents do if their child can't read easily?

The first step is to recognise the problem. It will no longer be necessary to put it all down to laziness or to assume your child is just being stubborn or isn't motivated to learn. Sometimes this comes as a great relief to a pre-teenager who has been blamed for so long by everyone for not trying.

The next step, with the school's advice and help, is to try to work out the reason why your child is having so much difficulty in reading. Can they resolve the problem at school? Is it part of a general difficulty in learning? Has your pre-teen missed out at a critical stage of schooling and needs remedial teaching to catch up? Is there a medical or visual problem that can be sorted out by discussion with a doctor, and perhaps a referral to a specialist? Is there the possibility that it is due to a specific learning disorder that needs expert sorting out and help? A specialist paediatrician, a psychologist or an educational consultant may be needed. Are there difficulties at home that are preventing your child settling down to learn?

All these possibilities need consideration. The school is the first line of help. If there is still no solution, perhaps discussion with your family doctor and referral to a specialist might be the answer.

Can anything be done to overcome a reading problem?

In almost all pre-teen children, the answer is yes. However, the longer it has gone on unrecognised, the more difficult it is to help the child as the difficulty becomes entrenched and the child gets frustrated. Many teenagers have given up the struggle, and couldn't be bothered to go through the painful process of relearning how to read. For others, it is a wonderful new opportunity. All pre-teens deserve the chance to learn to read with pleasure and ease.

The best way to help will depend on the reason why the child has had difficulty in the first place, and the extent that this can be remedied. This is why it may be so important to sort out the reasons for reading difficulties before embarking on programmes, tutors and remedial teaching that may not be appropriate for your child, however helpful they may be for other children.

There are now proven teaching methods available for poor readers to relearn to read fluently. They can work well with most pre-teens, and even teenagers. These methods are based on the time-honoured and basic methods of learning the sounds of letters and words. One of these methods is the Spalding method that was first developed sixty years ago, but has recently been shown in the USA and Australia to be highly effective as a way of teaching primary school children to read, and teaching older children and teenagers to overcome their reading difficulties. The method teaches the children to recognise the seventy basic letters and letter groups that are used to make the forty-five sounds that are in the English language. There are other equally successful methods that are based on the same principles.

To help understand the child's difficulty, and the methods that are now used to overcome them, try reading a newspaper upside down. You will recognise the common short words like 'the', 'and' and 'on' for example, but any words with more than a few letters will be very hard to recognise, and you will probably have to sound many of them out letter by letter to recognise the word at all. The fact that you are familiar with the words in everyday speech helps a bit, but it will still be a tedious and slow job making sense of a page. You might find that it has taken so much effort just working out the words, that when you have finished reading the page you can hardly remember what the newspaper article was all about.

If you could only read the print by recognising the whole word, and couldn't sound it out, you'd hardly bother to read it at all. This is just the difficulty facing many people who have never learnt to read fluently.

Whatever method is used to help pre-teens who have reading difficulties, it is important that they are given this opportunity to overcome their disability at this age, and not leave it until they give up altogether. It is becoming increasingly clear that success in tertiary education depends on reading and writing skills which should have been largely acquired well before the teenage years, and even people with manual trades need to be able to read.

Julian's problem was not an unusual one. According to a report to the Australian parliament in 1993, up to one in four Australian children entering secondary school now have severe reading, writing and spelling problems. No wonder so many teenagers hate school. Julian's mother was helping him find a solution before it got too late, and he said he was willing to give a programme of remedial reading a go.

Learning difficulties

'*I know he's not stupid. He seems quite bright in many ways, but he's having a lot of trouble at school, and I'm worried that next year will be very difficult for him when he goes to high school.*'

Mark had come along because the school said there may be something wrong. Just as his mother said, he seemed quite bright; he joined in all the class discussions and got on well with the other children at school. He could read fairly well, but he often forgot what he had just read out so clearly in class. The worst problem was that he didn't seem able to follow instructions. The teacher would tell the class to do something like opening their exercise book and copy notes from the blackboard so that they could write something about it for homework. She would find him dreaming away when the other children were busy, and he seemed quite confused when she confronted him.

As a result of his difficulties, he was getting further and further behind in his work, especially in maths.

His mother thought that the problem was that he didn't pay attention. She also found that he forgot things. If she told him to do a number of things for her, he might remember some of them, but he always forgot others. Sometimes he would start to follow her instructions, but she would find him halfway through what he had begun, wondering what on earth he had set out to do for her. Yelling at him didn't seem to help.

Mark had genuine learning difficulties, and his mother and his teacher were right: he wasn't stupid, but you might have thought so by the way he behaved in school and when he was asked to do things at home.

Children learn in different ways: by seeing, by hearing and by doing

Learning at school involves a series of complex processes. We all learn by hearing, by seeing and by doing. Some people are better at learning through what they hear. The teacher tells them things, and they can remember what they hear and can think it through. Others learn best through what they see. They read things from books or what the teacher has shown on the board, and remember what they see and can think this through. Some people learn best by doing practical things and they develop skills and knowledge that way.

Most children can learn through each of these methods. They are the lucky ones, because it can be relatively easy for them to learn in the classroom and at home. They learn through reading and listening; this is reinforced by writing notes and doing practical projects. Many children, however, may be good at one of these methods of learning, but less proficient at another. Some students may have trouble remembering much of what they are told in class, but if it is written down they cope well. Other children have so much difficulty in reading, and in recognising and remembering what they see, that they have to rely on what they hear. This will become a greater and greater problem for them as they get into their teens and are expected to rely on the printed word for much of their work.

Learning is a rather complex process

Learning also involves other processes. It depends on reasoning, on drawing on information already stored away in the memory, on expressing ideas in words, on getting things in the right sequence and not back to front. It relies on our ability to work out shapes and patterns and numbers. After all, the brain is like a very powerful computer. Sometimes there have been some gaps in the programming.

All students have relative strengths and weaknesses in how they learn

We think most students have strengths and weaknesses in the way they learn. Many will be able to compensate for their weaknesses through their strengths. If they have trouble in remembering what they hear, they learn to write down notes to remind themselves. Some may be able to do this to a certain extent, and get away with it in the early primary school years, but get into real trouble in secondary school. Others will have found school a struggle all along, but if they have been well behaved, and have contributed to class discussions and group activities, primary-school teachers and parents may not realise that their difficulties are as great as they are.

If a child is having difficulty in learning, we can usually work out why

It is possible to work out a child's strengths and weaknesses in how they learn, and any student who seems to be having difficulty should be assessed to check this out. Many teachers can do this, but in the ordinary classroom it may not really be possible as a child is one of a group and may need individual assessment. Most schools can arrange this with educational assessment, and parents should discuss this option with their child's teacher if there does seem to be a problem. Sometimes a paediatrician specialising in learning difficulties may be able to sort it out. Sometimes an educational psychologist will be the best person to do it.

Teachers sometimes feel uncomfortable in arranging for children to be assessed if they are having difficulties. Some are sure that all children can benefit from classroom teaching if only they pay attention and try hard. Some people feel that assessing a child's abilities may just show up weaknesses and make the child feel inferior. Other teachers are worried that although assessment might show up real learning difficulties for a child, this isn't helpful if the school hasn't the resources or ability to help them overcome their difficulties.

There are three answers to these objections to assessment. The first is that the assessment should show up strengths that can be used to learn, and not just demonstrate weaknesses that get in the way of learning. The second is that it isn't fair to blame a child for having difficulty in the classroom, or even for behaving badly, unless you understand why they are having difficulties. The third is that schools should be able to help children with difficulties, even in small ways such as where they sit in the classroom, or by giving them written notes, or extra time to complete tasks.

So the point in working out the reason why a child is having learning difficulties is that by knowing a child's strengths and weaknesses, the teacher can work through the child's strengths to overcome the weaknesses. Sometimes remedial teaching, particularly in reading and maths, may be very valuable, but in many cases there may not be much that can be done to improve specific weaknesses like a poor memory (though this often improves with time and the development of maturity).

Another good reason to work out why a student is having difficulties is that it may explain bad behaviour in class. A student who is quite bright may become very frustrated when they find that they have to struggle to learn what other students can do effortlessly. Their frustration may in time result in giving up trying altogether, or may lead to bad class behaviour. This is especially likely to happen in the teenage years, and is another strong reason to sort things out well before then, before it's too late to help.

Mark did have real difficulties as a result of some specific weaknesses in the way he was able to learn. He was unable to remember complex instructions or long pieces of information. If he was told several things at once he tended to forget half of what he was told, however much he tried. This is sometimes referred to as a poor short term auditory memory. It explained why he couldn't follow instructions if they contained more than two or three pieces of information. On the other hand, once he had learnt something he remembered it well.

By giving him information in small bits, making sure he understood these before going onto the next part, and by giving him written notes to remind him of what he was learning, Mark did much better and was very pleased when his next school report was good.

Getting organised with schoolwork and study

Some years ago a doctor specialising in adolescent health in America wanted to find out why some teenagers seemed very reliable, while others were unreliable, in taking medication when it had been prescribed for them. She gave a group of girls a little test. She asked them to consider two sorts of people. The first was Jane. She was very well organised. She never forgot her homework. She always thought ahead so she was well prepared for things. She knew where her things were. If she was sick and needed treatment, she always remembered her medication on time and finished the course of tablets.

The second was Sara. She was very different. She was very disorganised. She lost things because she forgot where she had put them. She was often late because she couldn't organise herself to get ready. If she got sick, she forgot her medication unless her mother reminded her, and she seldom finished the course of treatment her doctor had prescribed.

The group of teenage girls in the study were asked to say which girl they thought were most like themselves. Most were able to say exactly whether they were a Jane or a Sara sort of person. The research doctor recognised what every parent probably knows: some people are just naturally well organised, and some are not. It seems *to be part of their personality. The important conclusion from the study was that people who are naturally badly organised are most likely to be unreliable about important things like medication without a lot of reminding. The study also showed that most teenagers know quite well if they are naturally well organised or not.*

Being a disorganised sort of person is very common, especially in children and teenagers. It starts to be a problem in the pre-teens, because it is then that children are supposed to take some responsibility for themselves, especially in their schoolwork. When they were younger, their teacher would probably write notes in their school diary or send a message to parents if there was homework to be done or something had to be taken to school next day. Parents know they need to supervise and remind their small children; but when they get to their pre-teens, it's about time they learn to do some things for themselves. By the teenage years, the lucky ones have worked out some strategies to organise themselves. The unlucky ones get into more and more trouble at school, and probably drive their family mad.

It is easy to pick a disorganised pre-teen. They can't find things they need for school. They lose their locker key. They forget what they have to do for homework. They leave their diary at school, or they say they've lost it. They say there isn't any homework (when there really was). They leave school assignments until the night before they are due to be handed in.

Their school bag is messy. So is their school locker, with lots of things in it they have forgotten about. At home their bedroom contains piles of junk that they just step over, or around, and their desk has so much stuff on it that there is no room for homework books, so they move into some other part of the house where there is space. They often have difficulty getting started on their homework and put it off. Then they can't remember what it was they were supposed to do. It all gets a bit too much so they don't feel like doing it at all.

This is very annoying for their parents, but it is often just the pre-teenager's nature, and they have real difficulties in organising themselves no matter how hard they try. Sometimes a parent recognises a similar difficulty in themselves (or more often in their spouse).

On the other hand, there may be other more pressing things on the pre-teenager's mind, and these may get in the way of good work organisation. Their schoolwork may be so difficult that it seems better to think about something more pleasant.

Difficulty with organisation is common in children with Attention Deficit Disorder. They keep getting distracted from what they are supposed to be doing.

(See page 138 for a further discussion on ADD.)

Whatever the reason for being disorganised, their pre-teens is a good time to start developing strategies to overcome their difficulty. They may be able to develop good work practices before the teenage years, when things get to be much more complicated and distracting. It is also helpful to work out ways a parent can help their child without actually doing everything for them. It is probably just as big a worry for a child's teachers at school if they are badly disorganised with schoolwork, so it's an opportunity for parents and teachers to work together.

What parents might do to help a disorganised pre-teen

MAKE SURE THAT THERE IS A SUITABLE PLACE TO DO HOMEWORK
Preferably not next to the bed if they feel like flopping on the bed when it's homework time. Not in front of the TV, either, or in conflict with younger brothers or sisters who are a distraction.

COME TO AN AGREEMENT WITH YOUR PRE-TEEN ABOUT SET TIMES FOR HOMEWORK
Then make it a rule to stick to these times. Get them into a regular routine.

MAKE SURE LATE MEALS, PHONE CALLS, TV AND OTHER DISTRACTIONS DON'T INTERRUPT THE AGREED HOMEWORK TIMES

You may have to be a minder for your pre-teenager if friends make a habit of interrupting with phone calls or are in the habit of dropping by. They will soon get the message if you say 'Sorry, it's homework time. Can you call back later?'

GO THROUGH THE SCHOOL DIARY OR PLANNER

Do this together with your child at the start of homework time to help plan what should be done that day. Look ahead at assignment requirements and deadlines.

WORK WITH THE SCHOOL TO FOLLOW AGREED STRATEGIES TOGETHER

It will be helpful if you discuss with your child's teacher the best ways to work together to help your child become organised and achieve school requirements. Be careful that your child isn't getting conflicting suggestions at home and at school. Make sure the teachers know what your own strategies are so they can reinforce them and help make them work.

HAVE CHECK LISTS

Display them in prominent positions around the house to remind your pre-teen what to take to school.

DEMONSTRATE GOOD ORGANISATION AS A PARENT

Be a good role model, and show that it pays to be organised.

If these strategies don't work, consider whether there may be another reason why homework and study are so disorganised. For example:

- Is the schoolwork too hard, or is reading too difficult? There may be a real learning difficulty that your pre-teen is struggling with and which no-one has recognised yet.

- Has your pre-teen lost so much ground in a school subject that it is very hard to understand new work? This is particularly a problem with maths, where each step in learning and understanding depends on the previous one, and on the acquisition of basic maths skills.
- Does your pre-teenager have difficulty in maintaining attention and concentration? Are they distracted too easily ? It could be worthwhile to check whether they have Attention Deficit Disorder.
- Are there other things on their mind that get in the way of study and organised schoolwork? Perhaps there are emotional or social problems.

What the school might be able to do to help

These suggestions came from a group of schoolteachers who were studying ways of helping teenagers who had learning difficulties, and had trouble organising their work schedule. It might be helpful to discuss this with your pre-teen's teacher, in case they might be able to help.

1. Have structured lessons on 'how to be organised'. Lots of students would benefit, especially in year 7, at the start of secondary school.
2. Call the school diary a 'school planner' and teach the students how to use it; maybe have diaries out on the desk every lesson.
3. Write homework requirements briefly on the board or a piece of paper for each student who needs to take it home. Some students can't write down the requirements fast enough when details are given orally.
4. Have regular 'clean out your locker' sessions. Many students might be quite surprised at what they find in their locker — like things they thought they had lost.

5. If a student has a lot of trouble recording homework, the teacher could allocate a 'class buddy' to make sure that they have got it down.

6. Have check lists on the inside of the student's school folder, and lists inside their locker door with requirements for each subject.

7. Reward and acknowledge good organisation.

8. Provide opportunities for homework to be done at school. Many schools have a 'homework club' several afternoons a week after school.

9. Work with parents so they put planning practices in place at home.

10. Encourage use of a yearly planner. Form teachers or year coordinators might spend 5 minutes a week updating and discussing it with the whole class.

(These suggestions for schools were derived from 'Learning Links': Gabrielle Gardner and Ruth Fisher, Centre for Adolescent Health and Royal Children's Hospital School.)

Attention Deficit Disorder

Anthony had been known to his family doctor since birth. As an infant he cried a lot. His doctor sent him and his mother to a specialist who said it was colic, gave a medicine to help settle him down and advice to his mother about handling him. The medicine that was meant to calm him actually seemed to make him worse, and his parents got very little rest, as Anthony was always so full of energy.

As a toddler, he was very hard to manage. He had to be taken to the doctor on one occasion with bruises and scratches when he fell from a fence while trying to escape from the back yard. 'They probably thought I had bashed him, and to tell the truth, I could so easily have done so at times' his mother said. 'He seemed to have no fear of anything and you couldn't leave him alone for a minute.'

At kindergarten he was constantly on the go, wouldn't sit still and often fought with the other children. 'The kindergarten teacher suggested we should see a psychiatrist. When we did, he suggested ways to be good parents for Anthony, and obviously thought it was all due to the way we were bringing him up. This didn't help at all.'

When Anthony started school, he would wander around the classroom and wouldn't settle down for the teacher. By the third grade he was often sent out of class when he misbehaved. 'I think the principal got a bit sick of him,' his mother said, 'but actually he worked quite well when he was on his own with the vice-principal'. He was constantly distracted from any classwork, but he seemed quite bright in class discussions. The trouble was he often blurted out an answer before the teacher had finished asking the question, and he wasn't good at taking turns.

As he got older, his reports said his behaviour was poor because he tended to disturb the class. Remarks like 'Could do better if he would only concentrate on his work' started to appear on term reports. At the parent-teacher meetings, when he was in sixth grade, his teachers said they were worried that he might not cope socially with high school. They suggested having his eyes and his hearing tested, as he seemed to have so much difficulty in paying attention. His mother did this, but both vision and hearing were normal.

He was always losing things. He would argue for hours, even forgetting what he was arguing about ('That didn't stop him'). He had great difficulty in taking 'No!' for an answer to his many requests and demands. He seemed to be losing his friends, who were probably getting fed up with his rather demanding and often inappropriate behaviour in the schoolyard.

His family doctor and the school suggested that he should have intelligence tests, because he was getting such bad school reports, even though he seemed bright. The psychologist found that he was of average intelligence, although he had difficulty in completing some of the tasks that she set him. Nothing came of this, and Anthony's behaviour was getting worse.

Anthony's parents were getting very worried how he would cope with high school. When they heard from a friend about the condition called ADD, they decided to follow this up.

Anthony did have **Attention Deficit Disorder**. This is sometimes called **ADD**, but not all children show the same hyperactivity that Anthony did, and older children usually grow out of this aspect of the condition. The term **Attention Deficit Hyperactivity Disorder (ADHD)** is now used for children like Peter who have hyperactivity, but basically ADD and ADHD are the same condition. Although the features of ADD have been known to paediatricians for very many years, there was little that was understood about it. Initially, the main problem seemed to be a child's ceaseless activity, and the term 'hyperactivity' was used. Then, when it was found that the children who had been so active as toddlers were having learning and behaviour difficulties when they got to school, doctors thought they had some general brain dysfunction or damage. Because no cause could be found, such as a difficult birth, terms like 'minimal brain dysfunction' and 'minimal brain damage' were used for a time.

In recent years there has been a lot of research and enormous interest in the condition. Research has led us to understand more about the human brain: both in the way it works, and which part does what. Each part of the brain has specific functions, and we are starting to know what part is responsible for the skills and abilities such as attention and concentration that children with ADD lack. We are also finding that chemical substances (called neurotransmitters) are produced by the brain and how they are needed for it to function properly.

This has led to insights into how to help children with ADD, through understanding their difficulties, and then suggesting strategies for parents and schools to help care for them. Understanding some of the chemical processes that take place within the brain and help it function properly has also allowed us to give medication to those who have severe problems due to the condition.

What is ADD?

In spite of so much study and research, we don't really know exactly what ADD is or what causes it. What we do know is that it is a condition that affects many children and that they can respond to treatment. The term ADD is really a description of what some people think is the major problem: a difficulty in paying attention for long, particularly in learning and other tasks that require concentration. Hence the name 'Attention Deficit Disorder': a disorder resulting from a deficiency in ability to pay attention.

It has also been suggested that the real problem is a difficulty in persisting with learning and other tasks, so that although a child may start to do their schoolwork, after a short while they give up, and think of something else. They can't persist with the task until it is completed; or if they do finish it, it takes an enormous effort of concentration which they find very difficult.

We think that there is at least one part of the brain that has the responsibility of keeping our thoughts and attention focused on what we are doing. This is probably at the front and on the right hand side and is called the right frontal lobe of the brain. We believe that amongst other things it shields us from unnecessary distractions, either from things going on around us or from our own daydreams and other irrelevant thoughts and worries. With its help, we can do things efficiently and well and complete what we set out to do.

Of course, there are plenty of times that we can't really concentrate on what we are trying to do in our everyday lives. Perhaps the children are noisy, or we are very worried about something that is preying on our mind, or perhaps the task we are doing is very boring or too difficult, or we just aren't in the mood for it. Everyone experiences this at times. But children with ADD are like this most of the time, and often to a severe degree. It is difficult for them to maintain attention in class for more than a few minutes. They become distracted and think of something else or want to do something else. It is much harder for them in a noisy classroom than in a quiet room with just one person helping them, so they are often much worse at school or with a group of other children, but when a teacher has them alone, or a psychologist tests them out, they may perform quite well.

ADD most often first comes to everyone's notice when a child starts school, but it isn't just in the classroom that they have trouble. In fact, like Peter, children with ADD usually show signs of it even before they start school, and their difficulties aren't confined to school. Their parents see it in their behaviour at home, and in their inability to study. On the other hand, there are often strange inconsistencies about their behaviour. Sometimes children with ADD can play with video games for hours as if they are hypnotised by them. Sometimes they can do active things, like farm work or sport, without any trouble. Although children with ADD are often rather clumsy or uncoordinated, I have known quite a number of teenagers who are outstanding on rollerblades or at other physical activities.

One of the disconcerting things about children with ADD is their inconsistency. They may do something really well one day, but be hopeless the next day. They may behave very well for one teacher, but very badly for another. This leads to people thinking that they could do perfectly well, if they only put effort into it. Parents and teachers say 'You have shown that you can do it once, so there's no excuse for not keeping it up'. In fact, they usually can't put sustained and repeated effort into things when they have so much difficulty in maintaining concentration. Some teachers use techniques that are better suited to children with ADD, or are more understanding. An ADD kid will be much worse if he sits next to another one with ADD, but sometimes teachers put the troublemakers together at the back of the class so they don't disturb the others so much. ADD kids are better in a class setting that is well structured, and when work follows a regular routine. This may not be necessary for all children, but it certainly suits those with ADD.

Another unexplained thing about ADD is that it affects far more boys than girls, probably six times more often, although girls can certainly have it. But we know that boys are also more likely than girls to have other learning difficulties, and we don't know why this is true either. There is almost certainly a genetic factor in its development, as we often find that ADD runs in families, and there may be another sibling, a cousin or an uncle with it. I have often heard mothers say that they are sure that their husband has it too, and that this explains a lot in their husbands behaviour and why they clash so often with their ADD child.

What are the features of ADD?

Not all children with ADD have *all* the features of ADD, and certainly not to the same degree. Psychiatrists have constructed check lists for diagnosing ADD, but there are problems as many of the features can occur for other reasons. Quite often perfectly normal children display the same features to some extent. So, just because a child has some of these characteristics, to some extent, it doesn't necessarily mean that he has ADD.

There are three features that are always present in ADD

1. POOR CONCENTRATION
This makes children with ADD inattentive and easily distracted by things going on around them, or by their own thoughts. They often have a very short attention span, being only able to maintain attention for a few minutes, or remember short sentences when the teacher is speaking to them in class.

2. DIFFICULTY IN PERSISTING WITH TASKS
Children with ADD often fail to complete what they have set out to do. They may start something, but get quickly bored or distracted, and don't finish it. This gets progressively more of a problem as they get older, and when the school requires assignments and homework to be completed on time.

3. INCONSISTENCY IN WHAT THEY CAN DO
Children with ADD frequently seem competent one day, but may perform badly on the next. They tend to behave and perform

much better in a one-to-one setting than in a classroom or a group. This often is confusing when children have psychologist assessments or are given special tutoring.

There are a number of other features that are usually present

IMPULSIVENESS

Most children with ADD speak and act without thinking first. They may do things that are naughty, or dangerous, without pausing to consider the consequences. This often gets them into trouble at school because they may answer back to teachers, or behave badly in class and in the playground. They will often upset other children without really meaning to, through not thinking before they say something silly. They may lash out at someone who annoys them, and this may get them the reputation of being aggressive. As they get older, they may have difficulty in controlling their anger and lose their temper very easily.

INSATIABILITY

The is perhaps the most trying behaviour for parents of children with ADD. They go on and on if they want something, and won't accept no as an answer. They keep thinking of new things to support their demands. They can argue for hours, long after they have forgotten what the argument was initially all about. They need to be stimulated with new and interesting things, but quickly want to change to something else. They never seem to be satisfied.

SOCIAL CLUMSINESS

Children with ADD often have difficulty in maintaining friendships, sometimes because they find it difficult to read the small facial signs that people give when they are getting annoyed. Sometimes their difficulty in taking turns, an unwillingness to listen or their generally demanding behaviour starts to irritate their friends. The same is true in the school playground, and they may become quite unpopular. It may also lead to them being teased and sometimes bullied which makes it even harder for them to get on well with other children.

OVERACTIVITY

This is mainly a problem for parents of a preschool child, and seldom persists into the pre-teenage years. By this age, much of the wandering around has stopped, though they may wriggle and fidget a lot. But so do many other children. It is the extreme form that is sometimes referred to as ADHD, but some children even with ADD have never been particularly overactive.

DISORGANISATION

Some children with ADD are very disorganised. They leave things they need for school at home, and they leave things they need for homework at school. Their room is a mess, and they can never find things they want there. They lose things because they can't remember where they put them, or they get hidden under all the mess on their desk or in their locker at school.

Some children with ADD have associated problems

To make matters more difficult for children with ADD and their parents, some will have other problems that may make the diagnosis confusing, and which explain why usual management strategies may not always work.

Other learning difficulties

It has been shown that about half of children with ADD have other specific learning difficulties. These may be quite subtle, such as difficulty in appreciating spatial design or a poor memory for what they have seen. The difficulties are sometimes severe and are often quite critical for learning and may also include difficulties in remembering a sequence of instructions or difficulty in reading.

Older children, when they enter their pre-teenage years, may have missed out on learning things that they were perfectly capable of learning at an earlier stage, but didn't master because of their inability to pay attention. Perhaps they were sent out of class so often that they missed essential maths lessons, and now have difficulty with basic maths concepts. Perhaps they have such a bad reputation amongst their teachers that they don't always get the extra help they need. Perhaps they have had such difficulties in succeeding at schoolwork that they have become discouraged and given up trying.

Oppositional behaviour

About one in four children with ADD have some degree of what is termed 'oppositional behaviour'. They argue even when they have no excuse for it. They are often defiant even when they are clearly in the wrong. They may have temper tantrums even as a pre-teenager, and hit walls and kick doors when they are thwarted. They usually feel justified in their behaviour, even when it is clearly bad behaviour and they are disobedient. They may be cruel to other people, and seek revenge for things.

How can parents tell if their pre-teen has ADD?

There is no definite way that parents can be certain that their child's difficulties are due to ADD or not, but if their behaviour seems to match up with most of the above features, it would be well worth checking it out. After all, it has been estimated that probably at least 5% of all children have some degree of attention deficit, even though they may be coping quite well with it. Probably between 1 and 2% of children have it to the point that it is a real disability for them.

If parents think that their child might have ADD, they should discuss it with their child's teacher and their family doctor. They will need to be assessed by a specialist if the diagnosis is to be made and appropriate medication prescribed. Parents should recognise that not everyone actually believes that ADD really exists, and some professionals prefer to think that these children are just naughty or dumb. Modern research and current understanding however is clear: ADD may well be overdiagnosed sometimes, and there is much we don't know about it, but it is a definite condition and children who suffer from it deserve appropriate help.

How is ADD diagnosed?

At present there is no single test that can be given to diagnose ADD. The diagnosis is based on putting together all the information from parents, teachers and others who may have made assessments of the child. It will be necessary to consider all the other things that may influence a child's behaviour, such as emotional problems, visual and hearing difficulties, intellectual difficulties and underlying physical illness. The professional will need to check on associated learning difficulties that are so commonly associated with ADD, and at times may mimic the condition and confuse the diagnosis. The fact that a child has difficulty in paying attention doesn't automatically mean he has ADD.

Sometimes it is helpful to have formal psychological tests to achieve the diagnosis and to plan behaviour management. It can be helpful to have educational aptitude and achievement tests. There are some specific psychological tests that may help in the diagnosis, but the normal intelligence tests carried out by psychologists are not designed to make the diagnosis, and children often perform much better when they are being tested in a psychologist's office than when they are at home or at school.

It is possible that in the future tests on the brain, looking at how parts of it are functioning, will eventually become helpful in making a diagnosis of ADD. At present, these sorts of tests are only of interest as research investigations, and do not have practical value.

Although many experts in ADD consider that behaviour management should ideally be carried out by a group of professionals working with the family and child, this is not often practical or even necessary. It is, however, essential for the doctor advising on management strategies, and perhaps prescribing medication, to work together with the school and parents to help the child with ADD*. The first step is to get communication between everyone in place during the process of making the diagnosis.

What is the outlook for children with ADD?

In general, for most children with ADD the outlook, with appropriate treatment, is good. Some children will need medication and most children, but not all, will respond to it, some very well indeed. All will benefit from everyone understanding the difficulties, and from strategies to help them learn to control difficult and disabling behaviours. Many will need help throughout their school life, and some into tertiary education. Unfortunately, some will continue to have some difficulties into adult life, and a few will continue to need medication. But most will have learnt techniques to cope with their disability.

Strategies for managing ADD
(and other difficult pre-teenagers)

Some pre-teenagers with ADD respond well to medication, and some have such a mild problem that they don't need it. But all children and teenagers can be helped by management strategies that take into account their difficulty in paying attention for long and in controlling impulsive behaviour. These suggestions may also make it easier for members of the family with a pre-teenager who has ADD to live with less stress.

* I am indebted to Sydney psychologist Ian Wallace for his influence on my approach to the problem of ADD. For more information, see suggestions for further reading on page 209.

Medication is seldom enough by itself. What it may do is make it easier for the pre-teen and the teenager to make changes in their behaviour if they want to do so. Changes that the pre-teenager might want would be ones that help with behaviour at school and at home and lead to more success with schoolwork. Medication should be combined with a review of strategies both at home and at school that address the special needs of someone with ADD.

But don't expect a quick fix, particularly if there is a long history of school difficulties and failure; or if your child already has a reputation at school that is firmly entrenched and might take time to change.

REWARDS AND PUNISHMENTS

All young people need punishments to discourage bad behaviour, and rewards to reinforce good behaviour patterns. ADD children usually need a lot of rewards as well as punishments. With ADD children, the reward or punishment has to be quick or it won't have effect — they might have forgotten what it was for. Your response to bad behaviour has to be fairly immediate, and certainly while they are still thinking about what they have done wrong. If their concentration span is only ten minutes, that is the time limit you have in which to punish them.

This is also important at school. Response to bad behaviour should also be swift, but it is usually best if it is also brief. If a pre-teenager is sent out of class for bad behaviour, they will usually cool off in a few minutes, and then they could come back. If they are excluded for the whole lesson, they might become resentful and forget what it was they did wrong. They also miss so much of the lesson that they get further and further behind, and behave even worse in the next lesson.

DON'T GO IN FOR ARGUMENTS WITH AN ADD PRE-TEENAGER

It isn't worth arguing with an ADD pre-teenager. They are very good at arguing. They enjoy it. They can't bear to lose an argument, and may go on and on, throwing logic to the winds and eventually forgetting what it was all about in the first place. You'll eventually give in or lose your patience (and perhaps your temper) and that suits the ADD pre-teenager fine.

DON'T REASON WITH THEM WHEN THEY ARE BEING BAD

If an ADD child is being bad, it seldom helps to reason with them. It's almost as ineffective as arguing, and it probably annoys them, they lose concentration in what you are saying and don't pay attention. This won't help your peace of mind. Save the discussion for when they are settled and reasonable.

DON'T TELL THEM THAT YOU ARE 'REALLY UPSET BY WHAT YOU ARE DOING ...'

An ADD pre-teenager might love you and not really want to hurt you, but they can get satisfaction in annoying you, or provoking a response. If you say that you are really upset by something that they are doing, they may think that that's good (and do it again).

HELP YOUR PRE-TEENAGER BECOME SUCCESSFUL AT SOME THINGS AND DEVELOP SOCIALLY

ADD pre-teenagers often seem to be failing at everything — at school, socially and at home. As they do so, their self-esteem is becoming eroded and their social supports may be failing them at a very critical time in their life. All pre-teenagers need social and personal support. If they don't seem to be getting it, it might be helpful for you to look around. Discuss it with their school, your child's doctor or a counsellor. Help them to become engaged in something they can enjoy with other people. Consider non-team sports, youth groups, rollerblading, art or music.

TELL YOUR ADD PRE-TEENAGER THINGS BRIEFLY AND REPEAT IT ONCE OR TWICE; IF THEY DON'T SEEM TO HEAR, ASK THEM TO REPEAT WHAT YOU JUST SAID

ADD children often don't seem to be paying attention (they probably aren't, and maybe they can't). If you want to tell them something, and particularly if you want them to do something, speak briefly — repeat it once or twice to get their attention. They may not be listening the first time, but three times is quite enough. You may need to capture their attention to start with, then be brief and ask them to tell you what you just said if they seem to have been distracted while you were talking to them.

USE ROUTINE IN FAMILY LIFE, AND HELP THEM TO PUT STRUCTURE IN THEIR DAILY ROUTINE

ADD pre-teenagers respond best to firm routine and structure. They become even more disordered if things around them are in chaos. This particularly applies to homework, mealtimes, household chores and bedtime. An ADD child shouldn't sit anywhere near another ADD child at school.

MAKE RULES AND ABIDE BY THEM

Pre-teenagers can then argue with the rule instead of with you. They will probably say that the rule sucks. But as far as you are concerned, tough: 'No argument, sorry, that's the rule'.

ADD pre-teenagers need rules. Once the rules are clear and laid down, any argument is with the rules, not with you. It helps you to avoid long discussion and arguments. You don't have to respond to all their promises, threats and explanations: you just say 'Sorry, that's the rule.'

BE AWARE THAT SOMETIMES ADD PRE-TEENAGERS HARDLY REALISE WHAT THEY ARE DOING

Sometimes when ADD pre-teenagers are being particularly annoying they hardly seem to know what they are doing. It may be necessary to ask them what they are doing, rather than give reasons why it is wrong. When it is clear they are breaking an agreed rule, they can be reminded about the appropriate rule.

AVOID DELAYED PUNISHMENTS — MAKE THEM SWIFT

Delayed punishments may not work well as a deterrent. Stopping them from going to a party next weekend, or losing a privilege some time ahead, may be unhelpful. The ADD pre-teenager may have forgotten what it was all about by the time a punishment takes place. It may just make them angry and unbearable or not conform to the punishment. Ideally, punishment should be swift and soon over. That is not to say that they should be let off for really bad things, or that they should be given lesser punishments than the other children. It is the timing of the punishment that can be critical.

DON'T IGNORE ADD PRE-TEENAGE BAD BEHAVIOUR

If you ignore pre-teenage bad behaviour, they may turn to something even worse in an effort to get a more satisfying response from you. Respond quickly.

TURN CONSEQUENCES OF THEIR ACTION BACK TO THE ADD PRE-TEENAGER

Sometimes it is helpful to turn the consequences of bad behaviour back to the ADD pre-teenager. 'You decided to do this, so … ' 'You broke the rule, so … '

MAKE GOOD USE OF THE GOOD TIMES

All ADD pre-teenagers are good sometimes. Acknowledge these good times. Use these times to let them know how pleased you are with them. You can also reason more effectively with them when they are being good.

MAKE SURE THAT LEARNING DIFFICULTIES ARE HELPED, BOTH AT SCHOOL AND AT HOME

Very many ADD pre-teenagers have learning difficulties, particularly with reading. This can be very frustrating for them. Perhaps their difficult classroom behaviour has meant that their difficulties haven't been properly addressed.

These suggestions may work with some teenagers with ADD, but not all. Other factors complicate the issue, such as family problems, poor self-esteem, emotional problems and additional learning difficulties that compound the problem and will prevent the usual strategies from being fully effective.

Medication for ADD

The rationale for giving medication to children with ADD is this: the brain acts like a computer in many ways, but its function depends on chemical substances called neurotransmitters. Neurotransmitters help transmit messages between nerve cells, which are called neurones. Neurones are the basic units of the nervous system, including the brain. These neurotransmitters ensure that messages are sent through the nervous system in an orderly and efficient way.

We believe that in ADD some of these neurotransmitters are not functioning properly. It seems likely that the brain is not making them efficiently, or in sufficient quantity. What we do know is that it is possible to increase the efficiency of these neurotransmitters through stimulating them by medication. This seems quite logical, and there is ample experience to show that this stimulant treatment is one that works in most cases, and is safe.

The drugs that seem to stimulate these neurotransmitters are sometimes called psychostimulants. There are two forms of psychostimulant medication available at present in Australia: Ritalin (methylphenidate) and Dexamphetamine. These are far and away the most effective drugs for most children with ADD, but there are other medications that work in different ways that may be helpful in some cases, such as clonidine and some of the antidepressants. They work in a different way to the psychostimulants and may sometimes be used in combination, particularly in older children in their teens.

In Australia there are strict regulations for prescribing the psychostimulants Ritalin and Dexamphetamine. In most States they can only be prescribed by certain specialists, and special authority is needed to do so. This is because it has been felt that the medication might be used unnecessarily or even abused, and if so this could lead to dependence. There is no risk of dependence, however, when these drugs are prescribed and used properly for children with ADD.

Before considering medication, the specialist will need to be satisfied that the child really has ADD and not some other cause for their problems in learning and behaviour. It is, of course, important for both parents and the pre-teen to understand what the medication is attempting to do, how it works and the possible side effects. As the medication treatment for ADD is not a life-saving treatment (although some mothers would probably disagree with this as far as they are concerned), the final decision must rest with the parents and the pre-teen.

WHICH CHILDREN WILL BENEFIT FROM MEDICATION FOR ADD?

Medication should probably be reserved for those children who have significant problems at school stemming from ADD, and which have not been resolved by other measures. Of these, between 70% and 80% of ADD sufferers will be improved by one or other of the stimulants. Of those who don't respond, some will be helped by one or other of the other medications available.

It is not possible to tell in advance who will respond to medication and who will not. Some children will respond better to one form, and some to the other. Some children will have side effects with one form, but not with the other. This means that once the decision has been made to try the stimulant medication, it is often necessary to trial them and proceed to give one, and if there are problems, to try the other. On the whole, most specialists would consider that Ritalin is the preferred drug to start on, especially for pre-teens and younger children, but until now it has had the disadvantage that it is expensive.

WHAT CAN WE EXPECT THE STIMULANTS TO DO?

The stimulants Ritalin and Dexamphetamine help that part of the brain responsible for concentration and attention to function better. They help the child to concentrate better and to pay attention for longer periods of time. They are not sedatives, but they often make the child calmer and more focused on what they are doing. The child becomes less easily distracted from what they are doing, and thus may distract and disturb others less. They may also help control impulsive behaviour.

These stimulants only act for a few hours, and then rapidly pass out of the system. This means that most pre-teens will need to take their medication at breakfast time, and again at lunchtime. Some may even need a small dose after school to help with homework, or to help the bad behaviour that often plagues families of ADD children when they return from school and let off steam (this can be a 'rebound' phenomenon when the medication wears off at a time when children can be pretty trying anyway).

The cooperation of schools will be needed for supervision of the tablets. Sometimes pre-teens feel self-conscious about taking medication at school, in case they get teased, and teachers need to be sensitive about this. It's hard to resist the comment 'Have you had your tablet today, Peter?' whenever an ADD child misbehaves. I sometimes call the stimulants 'concentration pills' that only the best kids are allowed to have.

HOW SAFE ARE THE STIMULANTS?

Dexamphetamine has been used for children with ADD for over fifty years, and there is no evidence that it has led to dependence or addiction. Both Ritalin and Dexamphetamine have been highly researched, and long-term harmful effects have not been found. These medications are now so widely used, particularly in USA, that there is considerable experience over many years in their use and confidence in their safety. Having said that, it must be also said that any drug can be misused or given improperly, and it is essential that any child having medication should be checked regularly.

WHAT ABOUT SIDE EFFECTS?

There are some side effects that may occur with the medication but usually settle down quickly and seldom last more than a few weeks at most. These include some loss of appetite. With careful introduction of the tablets in correct dose, children usually notice very little change, and the effect wears off in time for the evening meal. Dexamphetamine may lead to some difficulty in getting to sleep, but only if the tablet is taken rather late in the day. Sometimes, in my experience, children get an occasional headache or abdominal pain in the first few days, though these don't persist.

Sometimes pre-teens and teenagers can get rather depressed when they start the medication. In younger children this is seldom a problem, though they can be rather emotional at first. Older teenagers may become quite depressed, perhaps because the tablets make them focus on their past failures and faults. Depression is perhaps the most significant side effect of stimulant medication at this age.

Side effects, if they occur at all, usually wear off in a few weeks, and are less likely to occur if the tablets are started at low dosage.

It has been reported that the stimulants may slow down growth. This should not be a problem if the medication is used properly, but we always monitor growth with any medication given to children. It has been shown that even if growth has been slowed, children catch up later, and adult height is not effected.

These and any other possible side effects of medication should always be discussed with your child's doctor.

OTHER FORMS OF MEDICATION

There are other forms of medication that are sometimes used in ADD, usually in addition to the stimulants. Some are more effective for pre-teenagers who tend to be confrontational and whose argumentative and aggressive behaviour isn't adequately helped by the stimulants. Antidepressants are sometimes helpful, but all drugs need full discussion and careful monitoring by your pre-teenager's specialist.

There is also the worry that an ADD pre-teenager may experiment with other drugs, including alcohol while they are having prescribed medication. Discuss this also with your child's doctor.

NOT ALL PRE-TEENAGERS WITH ADD NEED MEDICATION

For children with relatively mild ADD, it is often enough to use behaviour strategies that help them adjust to their disability, and to assist their school use techniques to overcome their difficulties. After all, no-one wants to give children medication unless it seems really necessary. For children who are still having severe problems by their pre-teens, however, the most effective way to overcome their difficult behaviour and trouble with attention is through medication.

Solving their problems while you can

Good kids can do bad things

Alan and two other boys had got into trouble. They had gone to their school one weekend and broken into the canteen. They had done quite a lot of damage getting into the building, and had stolen some soft drinks and packets of chips. The police had caught them soon afterwards in the park eating and drinking their ill-gotten gains.

Alan's mother was very upset. She couldn't believe that her son would have done this. It must have been his friends who made him do it. They were a bit older than him, and she had never approved of them.

'Anyway,' she said, 'it wasn't as if he didn't have his pocket money; he could have bought the chips and drink if he had really wanted them.'

'I didn't have any money' said Alan, who was looking rather ashamed and miserable.

'That's because you spent it on cigarettes!' his sister said, which didn't make the situation any better for Alan.

'I can't understand why he did it,' Alan's mother told me. 'And why did they have to go and damage the school?'

The reason that Alan had been brought along was because his mother thought it was so out of character. His father was disgusted and wanted him to be severely punished, but his mother wondered if there was some problem that had led him to do something so serious as breaking into the school. He may have got in with a bad group of friends who were older than he was, but he had always been brought up to be truthful and honest. Was there something troubling him that he couldn't tell his parents because they were so angry with him? Was it linked with trouble at school? It was his first year at high school, and he had been having trouble making friends there.

Doing something bad doesn't mean that a child is a bad person — good kids sometimes do bad things

Of course, all children and pre-teens sometimes do naughty things. Some are naughty rather often, perhaps because they have a mischievous nature and get a lot of fun out of testing their parents' patience. Some are impulsive by nature: they tend to do things without thinking of the consequences, such as whether they might hurt themselves or other people, or disappoint their parents. Sometimes this can be linked to hyperactivity and short attention span, and in a severe form may be part of Attention Deficit Disorder. *(See page 138 for a discussion on ADD.)*

Some haven't learnt to control their natural impulsiveness, perhaps because they haven't learnt through consistent rules for behaviour at home. Perhaps these rules haven't been reinforced by rewards for good behaviour and punishments for bad behaviour. Children do tend to follow their instincts unless they have firm guidance from their parents, particularly if each parent disagrees with the other about rules and punishments.

But when it comes to the pre-teenage years, it may mean that something more worrying is underlying the bad behaviour, particularly if the bad behaviour is uncharacteristic for the child. Sometimes a pre-teen is really troubled about something that they can't easily express in words to their parents, but acting badly may be a way of expressing that trouble. Pre-teens aren't always very good at telling people if something is worrying them, and they may not even understand what it is that is making them anxious, angry or sad. Doing something bad may be a signal to tell people that all is not well in their lives.

Pre-teenagers may not see it this way, of course, and may even think that they don't want their parents to help. But that doesn't mean that they aren't needing help. And subconsciously they are probably really wanting help. This is more likely in pre-teenage than in teenage years when things get more complicated socially and psychologically for them, and they may really resent any interference from their parents. And most teenagers who get into trouble have given warning signs of this when they were in their pre-teens. So this is the best time to act.

What might be underlying bad behaviour?

TROUBLE AT SCHOOL

Sometimes school becomes a burden for pre-teens. Most children enjoy primary school, both because it's fun learning and for the enjoyment of being with other children. It's even better if they like their teacher, and most do. But, by the age of eleven or twelve, some children are finding learning is difficult. By then they should enjoy reading, and they need to read to progress with their schoolwork. If they find it hard to read (and it has been estimated that in some schools, up to 25% of children do find it hard) schoolwork becomes much less fun. Also by then, children need to have a good grasp of basic maths skills. If they don't, maths will be a misery, and they will probably become convinced that they are dumb.

TROUBLE WITH FRIENDS

Friendships are seriously important for pre-teens and teenagers. Friends are important for everyone's happiness, but especially in the pre-teens, when social interaction becomes increasingly part of a child's development. At school it can be very lonely for a child who doesn't belong to a social group or have a best friend. Children can be very cruel to each other, and the most hurtful thing that can be done is to exclude a child from a social group. Sometimes a pre-teenager, who is rejected by the group of friends they would like to be with, seeks out any other child who doesn't reject them. It is so important to belong to a group, and it is so important to have a best friend, that it doesn't matter too much who that friend is and it doesn't matter too much what that group does, so long as the pre-teen is accepted by them.

Sometimes, if they are to belong to a group, a pre-teen has to do things with the group that they know is wrong. Sometimes they feel that they have to buy friendships by giving their friends things that they can't really afford: they might have to steal from their parents to get the money they need to buy these things. Sometimes they have to do things they know are wrong just to conform to the group behaviour, like shoplifting, smoking or glue sniffing. It's worth it just to belong to a group and not be left out of everything.

They may feel that their parents wouldn't understand this. Adults would only think what they were doing was wrong, and that the pre-teen deserved shame and punishment. Then they would be even more miserable, and perhaps resentful.

TROUBLE AT HOME
Pre-teens often worry a lot about what is going on at home. They may feel unhappy if their parents argue, and worry that they might split up. Perhaps there is more fighting and rivalry between siblings than the pre-teen can cope with. Sometimes children feel that they just don't belong in their family.

LOW SELF-ESTEEM
Even though they may love their child dearly, parents sometimes think that their child is a bit of a disappointment to them. This can rub off onto the pre-teenager, who feels the same way about him- or herself. Some parents have high expectations for their children at sport or school that pre-teenagers feel they can't live up to. They might feel that they are letting their parents down. They can feel that they are just no good. What's the point of trying? What's the point of being well-behaved if it means that your friends think you are a geek or a woos?

EMOTIONAL STRESS
Pre-teenage and teenage children who are depressed often act badly. They may be sad inside, but their behaviour is so bad that no-one

notices how they really feel. Angry children also can act out their anger with bad behaviour, often directed at other people or possessions. They may kick doors and punch walls or throw their books and clothes around their room. Parents don't always recognise that their pre-teenager's bad behaviour reflects emotional distress.

What can parents do about bad behaviour?

Management of inappropriate behaviour is, of course, one of the great challenges for parents. Some children, especially when they are small, hardly give their parents any cause for worry. Some seem to be getting into trouble all the time, and the only time that parents can relax is when the child is asleep. There are some general guidelines that may be helpful if a pre-teenager is consistently badly behaved, or if they do things that are really out of character and against family standards.

ACT QUICKLY TO GIVE PUNISHMENT IF IT IS DESERVED

Pre-teenagers know quite well that they need to be punished at times. It is usually best if the punishment is given quickly, because if it is delayed the child might think that the incident should be over and it isn't fair to punish them for something that happened so long ago (like yesterday or last week); especially if they have been trying hard to be good since then. For some pre-teens it is enough just to show that you are disappointed in them for what they did. For others, this is like water off a duck's back and they might even feel that it was a bonus if their parents actually suffered a bit. For them it has to be a punishment that hurts in some way (like grounding or a short ban on television or football).

DON'T ALWAYS PROTECT PRE-TEENAGERS FROM THE CONSEQUENCES OF THEIR ACTIONS

Parents naturally want to protect their children, but sometimes it isn't in their best interests if it means that they don't learn from their misdeeds. Sometimes they should just learn to live without some possession they have destroyed in a rage. They may need to pay back money they have stolen or pay for the repair of damage they have caused, even though it may mean that they have to get a job to do it, or use their pocket money.

Sometimes, if they have done something serious like shoplifting or damage to property and they have broken the law, it is very helpful for a pre-teen to be confronted by police. The police, especially community police, are usually very helpful in talking to a pre-teen about the consequences of doing bad things, and the risks they are taking in breaking the law. Most first offences at this age (unless they are very serious) result in a warning by police.

TRY TO WORK OUT IF SOMETHING IS TROUBLING YOUR PRE-TEENAGER

Consider the possible reasons why your child may have done something bad, especially if it was serious or repeated. It usually helps a child just to discuss their problems with their parents, even if they can't be resolved all at once, and it might take some time and effort to do so. Sometimes it is reassuring to them if you show that you know about their difficulties in growing up.

Perhaps doing something bad has been a blessing in disguise, because it has helped you to understand your pre-teenager, and it has helped them to know that you understand them better. However, sometimes it is useful to get professional help to achieve this.

Some behaviours should always be taken seriously

Some things that pre-teenagers do should always be taken seriously and probably need professional help. These things include repeated stealing, fire lighting, cruelty to animals and weaker children, bullying, damaging other people's property, inhalant sniffing (including glues and aerosols) and inappropriate sexual behaviour.

If you were worried about any of these you should discuss them with your doctor.

What about Alan? It was clear that he was having trouble making friends at school. He had got in with a group of boys who were troublemakers, and Alan felt he could only keep in the group if he did some of the things they did, even when he knew that it was wrong.

Alan's mother talked things over with the school counsellor, who arranged to meet Alan from time to time to talk about strategies for making friendships. Alan also joined a youth group where he felt more comfortable with a new group of children his own age.

Teasing and bullying

Melinda had reached a point when she didn't want to go to school. She begged her parents to send her to another school, even though her school was nearby and she had always liked her teachers there. She spent a lot of time crying when she was at home, and told her mother that she was getting teased all the time by a group of girls who had made her life a misery. To top it all off, the group had told everyone that they should refuse the birthday party invitations that she had sent to all the girls in her class.

Clearly Melinda was being bullied by a particular group at school, led by one or two girls. The teasing had become very cruel and hurtful.

Teasing, when it becomes malicious and repeated, is a form of bullying. Most children get teased a bit sometimes, and most cope with it quite well. They can give as good as they take, or laugh it off. Many children who tease others are looking for a chance to feel superior, or just want some fun at another's expense. A few hope to make themselves more popular by getting others to join in the teasing. If they don't succeed in getting others involved, or if their victim seems to treat it as being rather pathetic or all as a joke, teasers get bored or just give up. But bullies tend to go on and on.

Some children seem to have the knack of finding victims who will get upset by teasing. They seem to be able to induce others to join in the teasing so that they can feel superior. Teasing may then get to the stage of bullying. Bullying can be by word or deed, emotional or physical, and in many ways emotional bullying can be more cruel than physical violence, and harder to deal with.

Most people think of bullies as people who physically hurt their victims, and this certainly happens. Occasionally a child may be quite badly hurt this way, though bullies usually stop short of actually causing physical damage in case they get caught. They reason that a few bruises or a bloody nose could happen to any boy in the schoolyard. Bullies often justify their activities by saying 'They deserved it' but, of course, no child ever deserves to be bullied. Some children do seem to invite teasing, by the way they behave or boast stupidly for example, or when they refuse to join in activities. But that is no excuse to bully them.

Bullies aim to use power over another child. They may do this by hurting or intimidating them. They may use teasing, name calling, spreading rumours, making nasty gossip or excluding a child from a friendship group. They may damage or steal another's personal property (especially things that the other child may really value or need), or they may physically hurt them or humiliate them. Occasionally, a child may be coerced into giving money to their bully or to do something that they think is wrong, such as stealing. Sometimes bullying may be quite subtle, such as refusing to share something like a ruler or a book. Isolating a child at school is one of the most cruel and hurtful ways of group bullying, and sadly it appears to be quite common, particularly amongst girls. Sometimes a group of children will just stop chatting to each other when another child approaches, making it clear that she is not welcome to join the group.

Schoolteachers often don't know about the bullying or excessive teasing that occurs in their class. There are times when children are not being supervised or watched by teachers, such as in the playground or in the toilets. Sometimes bullying is so subtle, such as the spreading of cruel rumours about a child or isolating them socially, that it would be very difficult for a teacher to know about it unless someone told them. In many schools, telling a teacher or dobbing in a fellow student is very much frowned on by other students, and even by the teachers themselves.

All this can be even more painful when a child reaches the teenage years, so it is important for parents and schools to tackle the problem, when they get to hear about it, in the pre-teens, and deal with it as soon as possible.

What can parents do about teasing or bullying when it affects their child?

Parents should encourage their pre-teen to talk about it, and not feel ashamed: it's not their fault, and it's important to do something about it. They must feel that they don't have to put up with it and, as a parent, you are going to help.

The school must become involved

In any case of bullying, the school must become involved. Bullying in schools is much more common than teachers had previously thought, and studies in England and Australia suggest that it can occur without teachers knowing about it or realising how serious it is. It can occur in any school, even in schools where teachers are caring and friendly.

If it seems serious, and not just a brief fight with some of their classmates, it is essential that parents talk to the school about it. In primary school the class teacher should be told, and if this doesn't seem to be helpful the parents should see the principal or vice-principal. In secondary school, parents should talk to the year coordinator or the student welfare officer. Some schools have a pastoral care director. It is seldom sufficient to leave it just to a school counsellor (although if there is a school counsellor, they may be very helpful as well) as it isn't a problem for the victim alone, but also for those doing the bullying and for the school itself. It's important for parents to do this, both for their child and for others who may also get teased and bullied.

There are some very helpful guidelines available for schools to help overcome bullying. The school must make it very clear that bullying is not tolerated and is against school philosophy. Parents of the students who are doing the bullying must also be involved. It is not fair for the children who are being bullied to have to cope with it all by themselves.

If the bullying is taking the form of isolating the child, excluding her from friendship groups, it is just as important for the school to become involved, even if there isn't any physical or verbal violence.

The child who is being bullied must be given clear support both at school and at home. Sometimes it is possible to have an older child at the same school become involved as a buddy, perhaps by just having an odd chat or friendly word in the schoolyard. It is essential that this older student is one who is held in high regard by the other students, as this gives the child who has been bullied some status. It usually helps them to know that another student, and not just their parents, is on their side.

You can't ignore teasing or bullying

It isn't very helpful to tell your child to 'just ignore it'. How can you possibly ignore someone who is deliberately trying to hurt you? Or a group who are excluding you? A child could probably only do this with the help of friends who are in their class. A child who is part of a strong group of other students may be able to turn to them for support, as bullies don't set on a whole group as a rule. But most children who get teased or bullied feel very much alone.

Here are some things that may be worth trying

HELP YOUR CHILD TO GET A GOOD FRIEND
Everyone at school needs a best friend. Sometimes it's very hard if a child is rather unpopular, as most other children who might have been friends won't want to become associated with someone who is being teased. But it is worth trying, and if your child identifies someone who is friendly, make sure that you give opportunities for them to be asked around after school or on the weekends to develop the friendship.

TEACH SOCIAL SKILLS
This might include showing how to share things with friends, or how to take a joke even if it does seem to be a bit hurtful. Some children find it hard to start conversations and need suggestions, such as talking about a current TV soapie, a sporting star or current band on the radio.

PUT TEASING IN PERSPECTIVE
This way it doesn't seem to be such a disaster.

HELP YOUR PRE-TEENAGER TO DEVELOP PERSONAL STRENGTHS
What things is your child good at? Give lots of acknowledgment for any skills and successes so that self-esteem is preserved.

GET YOUR PRE-TEENAGER INVOLVED IN SOME OUT-OF-SCHOOL ACTIVITY
Some possibilities are a youth group, scouts or guides, karate, netball with a club, rollerblading or skateboarding. It is good for them to be part of a group they are doing things with and who don't tease them.

GIVE SOME STRATEGIES TO RESPOND TO TEASING OR HURTFUL REMARKS

Your child might say something short and smart, such as 'Very clever!' or 'Very original!' or 'You should know!' and then turn away. No extended arguments or long denials. Just a quick retort and your pre-teen can then walk away or turn to someone else.

IDENTIFY 'TRIGGER FACTORS'

These are things that your pre-teenager might do or say, or situations that may start the teasing. If you and your child can work this out, they might be able to minimise the times when teasing starts.

REHEARSE SITUATIONS AT HOME WHERE YOU ARE BEING TEASED BY YOUR CHILD

Suggest ways you might respond. Introduce humour, so that the bully looks silly. Maybe your child could imagine that the teaser has a green nose, or her shoes are back to front, or his pants have fallen down. They might lose some of their power over your child.

HAVE YOUR CHILD KEEP A DIARY OF THE TEASING OR BULLYING

Have your pre-teen write down what started it off and how they coped. A day without teasing gets a star. An occasion when your child coped with it well gets a gold star! If there has been a bad day, it might give you a chance to discuss how they might have coped better. Your child may find it encouraging when the teasing becomes less frequent. But remember: everyone gets teased sometimes.

If these things don't prove helpful, and if the school has done all it can to help, but there is still a problem and your child isn't coping well, get some professional help.

Melinda did change schools. She couldn't see how things could improve at her old school, even though the teachers wanted to help. Before starting at the new school, her parents made sure that she had learnt ways of making friends and keeping them. She also practised ways of coping better if she should be teased. She joined a jazz ballet group outside the school, made a friend there and worked hard preparing for a concert.

Lying: is it just a crime of childhood?

'*I can accept anything except her lies, Doctor.' Lucy's mother was telling me about her naughtiness and was wondering how she was going to cope when she became a teenager. 'If only she admitted she had stolen the money from me, I could have punished her and forgiven her. But she kept saying she didn't, and refused to admit it even when we found the comics she had bought with it.' She went on to say that the one thing she demanded from her children was that they tell the truth.*

Lucy told me she thought that telling the truth sucks, even though she knew she should not tell lies. 'If you own up to doing something at school you get a detention or sent to the principal or you even get suspended. But if they can't prove you did something, they can't do anything about it.'

Lucy's mother was right, of course. If your children can't be truthful with you, how can you trust them? And trust is so important in helping children grow up, especially as they approach their teens. But Lucy also had a point. It doesn't always seem to pay to be truthful, and experience suggests that there are many reasons for a child to hide the truth, some of them quite understandable.

Almost all parents try to bring up their children to be truthful. It's a great virtue, and all religions speak of truth as the basis of religion and belief. Children are told that it is really bad to tell lies. To be caught out telling lies makes you feel even worse. It's not just naughty, it's something to be really ashamed about. You've let your family down.

Children taunt each other when they are arguing: 'You're a liar', 'She tells lies' and 'You're lying'. If there's one thing that is liable to make a child burst into tears, or become furious, it is to accuse them of lying when they are not. They may not be able to prove to you that they are telling the truth (and they may have been lying before) but if they have been truthful on this one occasion, and you don't believe them, it is very frustrating and upsetting, and it makes them feel it is very unfair.

Everyone tells lies sometimes

A recent research study report of an interview with a teenager and her mother went something like this:

Mother: *'One thing you can say about her, she never lies.'*

Daughter: *'That's silly. Of course I lie sometimes. Everyone does.'*

Children know that other children lie, and they soon find out that adults do, too. Even the ones they love and trust lie sometimes. When they become a little older, and certainly as teenagers, they find out that lying is regularly practised, and even encouraged, by some people. If you commit a crime and the police accuse you, your lawyer will probably say 'Don't admit it. Deny it. Plead "not guilty" (unless you were actually caught red-handed)'. If you are a politician and want to get votes, you will make all sorts of promises that you know you can't keep, and you will probably deny all sorts of attacks and accusations made in parliament. Sometimes doctors and nurses might say 'This won't hurt' as they give you an injection, but then it really does hurt, and you realise they only said it to make you keep still, and it was a lie. Even parents might say 'If you do that once more I'll give you such a smack', but you know they won't. They are just lying to get you to stop doing something. Children learn a lot about adult behaviour by their pre-teens, and then they apply this to their own behaviour.

It can be confusing for a pre-teen to work out when to tell the truth and when to try to get away with telling a lie. As children become teenagers, they can get very inventive and convincing about their lies. Sometimes they get very angry if you catch them out lying. Sometimes their lies are so good that they convince themselves, and then end up thinking that they weren't lying at all.

But parents know that unless their pre-teen intends to lead a life of crime, it doesn't pay to live a life of lies. On the whole, and despite lots of evidence to the contrary, it ends up better if children and teenagers and parents all tell the truth. There have to be rules about trusting children to tell the truth that pre-teens can understand and try to stick to. They should be punished for lying, but they shouldn't be punished for telling the truth, such as when they own up to something that they shouldn't have done.

Pre-teens and teenagers should recognise that there are some important issues that the family must rely on them to be absolutely truthful about. This includes things that they have done that might endanger others or things that they know might hurt themselves or upset others. Also things that affect their health (such as not taking their medication if they are sick or have a health problem) and wagging school, or not telling their parents where they are going after school or at night.

So what can parents do to help their pre-teen to be truthful?

ALWAYS BE AS TRUTHFUL AS POSSIBLE YOURSELF
Do this even if the truth might seem to be painful for your child. Sometimes parents try to protect their children from hurtful truths, but when they get to the pre-teen years they usually find out, and then it is worse.

MAKE IT CLEAR THAT TRUST DEPENDS ON BEING ABLE TO RELY ON THE TRUTH ABOUT IMPORTANT MATTERS AT ALL TIMES
Family trust is the basis of living comfortably together and for pre-teens to start to develop independence.

RECOGNISE THAT EVEN GOOD CHILDREN DO NAUGHTY AND SILLY THINGS AT TIMES

They need not be too ashamed of being children and doing childish things, provided that they learn something from it. Hiding the truth from parents makes it hard to learn anything that is helping their development.

GIVE YOUR PRE-TEEN CREDIT WHEN THEY OWN UP TO DOING SOMETHING WRONG

When your pre-teen owns up to doing something wrong, especially if it is something that they are ashamed of, give them credit and make them aware that you are proud that they were brave enough to admit to it. That doesn't mean that they shouldn't be punished for what they have done if punishment is appropriate. Most pre-teens know that they deserve being punished sometimes.

DON'T GET TOO HUNG UP ABOUT MINOR LIES

Just make it clear that you know what is what. If your pre-teen thinks that the worst thing that could happen is for them to get caught telling lies, they might just get smarter and smarter at lying. And one thing that teenagers are generally expert at is hiding the truth.

Stealing: is it normal at this age, or a sign of something really going wrong?

A group of pre-teenagers were talking in the school playground after one of them had been caught shoplifting. She'd taken a game for her computer, and the police had been to see her and her parents.

'How did you get found out?' 'What did your dad say when the police came round?' 'Was this the first time you got caught?'

'What's going to happen to you?'

'My dad is really angry and has grounded me for a month so I can't go to any parties or see my friends after school or anything,' Michelle said. 'My mum tried to tell the police that I couldn't have done it and it would have been one of my friends who gave it to me. She seems to think that will get me off, but I don't know.'

'Is your mum really mad with you?'

'Well, she says she's disappointed in me, but she's mainly angry that the police came round and said that I might have to go to the Children's Court.'

Most pre-teenagers and young teenagers take things that don't belong to them at times. It might be a dollar from their mother's purse, a tape from their older sister or a pencil from someone at school. Few do it repeatedly; mostly they don't take large amounts of money or valuable things. Sometimes parents don't set a very good example themselves when they fail to return things they borrow or appropriate money or small belongings from each other, or other members of the family, without telling them.

Some parents think that stealing is just part of growing up and fairly normal at this age, and often it is. Others feel very disappointed in their child, who seems to have rejected all the moral values that they have tried to teach their children. When their child lies about what they have done, the crime is worse, and sometimes parents say that they would have felt a lot better and forgiven their pre-teenager if only they had owned up and hadn't lied about it.

How can parents tell when stealing is a serious problem for their pre-teenager?

Sometimes when pre-teenagers take something that isn't theirs, they feel ashamed and don't repeat it. Parents hope that their child will learn something from it, especially when they are found out and punished. They may have to earn the trust of their parents again, but no great harm has been done in their personal development, and parents will be able to forgive them and put the whole matter behind them.

Sometimes a child will learn the wrong lesson. If they aren't caught they may feel that stealing is easy and gets them what they want. If they aren't punished and made to realise that what they did was wrong they may never learn about honesty, trust and considering other people's feelings or how they might suffer. It might not just be the stealing that was the problem, but also the failure to take the consequences of the theft and learn from it.

But sometimes stealing is a sign of some underlying and serious problem for the pre-teenager. To check this out, some of the questions that parents might ask include:

- Does the stealing take place outside the home and the family?
- Does the pre-teenager steal repeatedly or is it just this once?
- Does the pre-teenager feel sorry about stealing (and not just angry that he has been caught)?
- Does the pre-teenager lie repeatedly about what he has done, even when there is no doubt about it?
- Does the pre-teenager justify theft by saying that they needed the money because they don't get enough pocket money? If so, this needs to be discussed, because every family has to live within a budget, including pre-teenagers. If the family budget doesn't allow them to have all they want, this may be something they have to live with, and it can be a valuable lesson for adult life.
- Does the pre-teenager say he knows it was wrong but he couldn't help it?

If any of these things seem to apply, it is better to seek professional advice before behaviour problems become entrenched in the teenage years. Most pre-teenagers welcome help if they know they have a problem. It's such a common problem that you shouldn't be embarrassed to discuss it with your family doctor or ask for referral.

What can parents do if their pre-teenager is found to be stealing?

IT IS USUALLY BETTER TO LET A PRE-TEENAGER SUFFER THE CONSEQUENCES OF WHAT THEY HAVE DONE
To protect them from any bad consequence, which would be a natural reaction for most parents, may mean that their pre-teenager doesn't learn any useful lesson from the incident. If the consequence is a stern warning from the police, so be it. If they have to pay something back, let them earn the money or pay from out of their savings; don't pay it for them.

DON'T ALWAYS GIVE YOUR CHILDREN EVERYTHING THEY WANT OR ASK FOR
They may become resentful if the time comes when you can't afford to give them what they think they need, or you feel that they shouldn't have it. As one fourteen-year-old compulsive stealer said to me recently: 'When I was just a kid, my parents gave me everything I asked for. But in those days it was usually just a little toy or something. Now when I see a Walkman or a computer game, I just have to have it, even though my parents won't buy it for me and I know I shouldn't steal it.'

MAKE FAMILY MORAL VALUES VERY CLEAR TO YOUR CHILDREN AT ALL TIMES
Most teenagers eventually come back to their family values as they grow older.

HELP THEM TO DISCOVER THE VALUE OF SAVING UP FOR SOMETHING THEY WANT
It isn't a very popular pastime these days, with credit cards and bank loans, but it is a valuable lesson for a pre-teen to put off

getting something they want, rather than receiving instant gratification of every wish.

TRY TO WORK OUT IF THE STEALING IS REALLY A SIGN OF SOME UNDERLYING EMOTIONAL PROBLEM
Are they otherwise happy, with good friendships, and succeeding at school? Do they seem to have good self-esteem? Do they cry a lot, or retire to their room for hours?

CHECK IF THEY NEED TO STEAL TO GET MONEY FOR SOME OTHER REASON SUCH AS:

- to get friends by buying things to give them (this seldom works)
- to be part of a group who might have more money than you can afford to give, or who have things your child doesn't have, but feels they need to belong in order to the group
- to buy cigarettes or drugs (sometimes this starts in the pre-teens)
- because they are being bullied into stealing.

Michelle eventually got a warning from the police, who were actually very helpful. She had a long talk to her parents, and agreed to go to the shop with them and apologise. She had returned what she had stolen, but as it was now used, she agreed to get a part-time job to repay the cost. Her dad said he was proud of the way he had acknowledged what she had done, but she still got grounded for a month!

Bedwetting

Chris wet the bed most nights; he just slept so deeply that he couldn't wake up to go to the toilet. To prove how deep a sleeper he was, he told me how he had woken up one morning in a blanket in the next-door neighbour's garden. During the night his house had caught fire. His father had picked him up out of bed, wrapped him in his blanket and put him safely in the next-door garden. Then he had coped with the fire and the younger children, and had forgotten all about Chris. Chris was pretty cross, because he had missed the fire brigade, the sirens and all the excitement. He had slept through it all. No wonder his brain didn't wake him up when he needed to empty his bladder!

Chris was aged eleven. He and his parents had more or less got used to his bed wetting, but there was a school camp coming up, and he didn't want to go while he might wet his bed there.

It has been estimated that one in ten boys wet their bed at the age of five, but most will have stopped by their teens. However, some teenagers still wet their bed sometimes, and it becomes much more socially embarrassing as they grow older. They may not feel happy about going to school camps, even though their friends are going. They will probably feel nervous about sleeping over at a friend's house, and it may be very hard to explain to their friend why they won't stay.

It's well worthwhile trying to stop bedwetting before they are teenagers. Most parents know that it isn't their child's fault, and it isn't due to laziness. Certainly if a child is frightened of the dark, it may be a big ordeal to get up in the night to go to the toilet, and a light in the passage may help. Most parents have tried various things, such as rewards for dry nights, limiting fluids before bed and waking them up during the night. Sometimes these tactics help. Mostly they don't. If they do help for a while, it may be that the child is making a superhuman effort of willpower, which they can't be expected to keep up. It may lead to disturbed sleep or perhaps they have come to rely on a parent getting them up.

Some children have never been completely dry at night, even though they have no trouble during the day. It is likely that this is due to a late development of that part of the brain responsible for bladder control. This is the most usual cause, and for some reason is much more common in boys. It is seldom due to an abnormality or to mental problems. Often it runs in families, so there is probably an inherited basis.

Certain children go through the usual period of becoming dry at night, but after a time start to wet the bed again. This may have a different cause, and it is usually wise to check it out with your doctor. It could as a result of emotional stress (such as problems at school), due to a bladder infection or even more serious reasons such as diabetes. When the cause has been found, and treated, the bed wetting usually stops.

For those children who have never got complete control of their bladder at night however, there are treatments that usually work, and which should be tried when the child feels ready. The most effective of these is one that 'trains' the brain to respond to the urge to pass urine while the child is asleep, and is sometimes referred to as 'conditioning'. In this treatment the child sleeps on a special pad that is sensitive to moisture and is connected to an alarm that sits beside the bed. It works on the principle that as soon as the child starts to wet, the pad sends signals to the alarm which wakes the child. It must be a reliable pad and alarm, and it only works if the child follows instructions carefully, often initially with the help of a parent. This is the first step in a process of teaching the brain to control the bladder automatically. After a few nights, the child finds he wakes up more easily when he starts to pass urine, and eventually either wakes up before he wets at all, or just sleeps through the night, waking with a dry bed in the morning.

Sometimes medication helps, either alone or in combination with the alarm system. See your family doctor to discuss this.

Chris decided he would give the alarm system a go. The first few nights it woke his mother (and the dog and one of his sisters) before him, and his mother had to get up to help. After a week he wet less and less often, and finally stopped.

Alcohol: when should they start?

'*We let her have a drink with us now and again. Just a sip or a small glass. We think it is good for our children to feel that they can drink sensibly. And anyway, we would rather they had a drink with us knowing about it than secretly.'*

Clare's mother and father were discussing their twelve-year-old. Their fifteen-year-old niece had come home drunk after a party recently, and Clare's parents hoped that they could prevent her drinking stupidly when she became a teenager.

I admired their optimism, but agreed that as their family drank alcohol in moderation regularly, then it was important for their children to learn to drink wisely, and know the family rules about drinking. All parents need to make their attitude towards underage drinking clear.

By the age of seventeen, 70% of both boys and girls at secondary school in Australia drink alcohol at least occasionally. Three per cent of boys and 2% of girls at that age are heavy drinkers, and 30% of boys and 21% of girls are what they consider moderate drinkers. Teenagers sometimes consider their drinking as moderate while their parents would think of it as quite excessive for good health and safety. Most children have their first drink in their own home, and usually with their parents' knowledge.

When do children start drinking?

At year 7 in secondary school, when most children are about twelve, 84% of boys and 88% of girls have not yet started drinking. This means of course that already 16% of boys and 12% of girls are drinking, at least occasionally. Over the next four years, more and more children will start drinking (not just to try it out with an experimental glass, but regularly). By age fifteen, 40% of boys and 37% of girls have started regular drinking.

Drinking alcohol has become very much part of teenage culture in Australia, and most people feel that although this is most unfortunate, and can be harmful both physically and socially, it is better to teach teenagers to drink wisely than to try to stop them drinking altogether. Many older teenagers resent their parents telling them what to do when they are at parties or with their friends. Anyway it might be rather too late to influence them. They probably won't be very impressed to know what it could be doing to their liver or to their brain or that they might be in danger of becoming an alcoholic and addicted to drink. As far as doing something stupid at parties or getting a hangover, they say that is what teenagers do anyway, so why worry?

For most families, the time to start helping children make sensible decisions about alcohol is in their pre-teens

It might be helpful to understand why some teenagers drink and some don't. Despite the repeated opportunities and pressures from other teenagers to drink, there are many reasons why many don't drink at all, or only very occasionally. There was a recent large survey of students in years 7, 9 and 11 at school. This showed that the most common reasons these students gave for not drinking were:

- that their parents wouldn't approve
- that it would affect their schoolwork
- and they couldn't afford it.

Almost half of nondrinkers at all ages say that they don't like the taste of alcohol, and that is why they don't drink.

Many of the teenagers who were nondrinkers said in the survey that they will drink when they are eighteen and it's legal. This legal consideration doesn't seem to influence most teenagers and no amount of house and school rules stop them from drinking as they get into their middle teens and find that most of their friends are drinking. It can become socially important to them, quite apart from the enjoyment of it all.

It can be confusing for pre-teenagers to be told not to drink because it isn't good for them, but then see their parents offering a drink to friends whenever they call round (so it is socially acceptable and even desirable). They may see their parents having a drink to unwind after a day's work (so alcohol makes people feel good and helps them relax). They may see parents having a drink of wine or beer with their meal (so it is part of normal daily living). They may see parents and other adults become funny and laugh a lot when they have had a few drinks (so it helps people have fun).

All these things that adults use alcohol for are fine. Why not for teenagers? Part of the answer is that the developing body will not have quite the same capacity to handle alcohol that the adult body has. The liver needs to break down the alcohol so it doesn't build up in the body. Too much alcohol puts strain on the liver, and can damage it.

How much is too much? We don't actually know how much alcohol is safe for a teenager or pre-teen, but even if it is quite safe from a medical viewpoint for a teenager to have one or two drinks, many don't know when to stop. We do know how much is safe for adults, and that men can safely have almost twice as much alcohol as women because of their liver capacity to handle it. This does not mean, of course, that men behave better when they drink: it only demonstrates the physical danger to men and women's health.

The most important reasons why we want to help young teens avoid the harm of drinking are the social and behavioural repercussions. Teenagers tend to take risks without thinking through the consequences, and alcohol increases these risks enormously. A large part of dangerous and violent teenage behaviour is under the influence of alcohol. Nearly 10% of seventeen-year-old boys and girls said in the survey that they had regretted having sex after drinking. Many found that they had little recollection of what they had done when they had been drinking with friends. Some found that they couldn't stop drinking once they had started.

The greatest worry is that it is very easy for some people to get addicted to alcohol, and the risk is probably greater if they start binge drinking early in their teenage years. You can't always predict who will become addicted. Sometimes children from families who drink only moderately become addicted. Often, however, susceptibility does seem to run in families; and if there is an alcohol problem in other members of the family, the risk is much greater for the pre-teen and young teenager. Most teenagers who drink do so mainly at weekends, and many binge on alcohol to the point of getting excessively drunk. The great concern is for those who find that they need to drink this way to enjoy parties, or cope with life's problems, or if they just can't stop drinking once they start.

These are the reasons why we want pre-teens to start thinking about their attitude towards alcohol. At this age they will want to know what their parents think about them drinking. They may need to understand good reasons why they should resist the temptations offered by friends and especially older children.

What can parents do to help their pre-teen make sensible decisions about drinking?

IF PARENTS THEMSELVES LIKE TO DRINK, THEY SHOULD SET A GOOD EXAMPLE
Parents should demonstrate the good aspects of alcohol if used in moderation in their own drinking habits. Pre-teens are very much influenced by the role modelling provided by parents.

IF SOMEONE IN THE FAMILY DOES HAVE AN ALCOHOL PROBLEM, TALK ABOUT IT
Most pre-teens who see violence (including verbal violence) in the home when one or other parent is drunk, become very distressed. Most will want to try to understand it and avoid it themselves. Some teenagers and young adults may end up with the same problem if it is not addressed in the pre-teenage years.

IF PARENTS DO NOT DRINK AND DISAPPROVE OF ALCOHOL, MAKE SURE THAT THE PRE-TEEN UNDERSTANDS WHY
It can be confusing for them to find that their parents have such strong views about something that their friends' parents feel very differently about. In Australia, only a small percentage of

teenagers avoid drinking for religious reasons, but these beliefs may be very important for them. On the other hand, a pre-teen might be very comfortable with their family's religious beliefs, but may still feel that the rules about alcohol can be challenged.

DECIDE IN ADVANCE WHETHER YOU INTEND TO PLACE AN ABSOLUTE BAN ON ALCOHOL IN THE TEENAGE YEARS, OR WHETHER YOU ARE HAPPY FOR YOUR TEENAGER TO DRINK IN MODERATION
Making this clear in the pre-teenage years will help maintain discussion later when they are teenagers. If parents do decide that drinking in moderation is acceptable for a teenager, perhaps they should take the responsibility to teach them to drink sensibly with the family at home, rather than confine their drinking to teenage parties, where they may very well get the wrong lessons.

REMEMBER THE REASONS THAT WERE FOUND TO MOST INFLUENCE PRE-TEENS AND TEENAGERS NOT TO DRINK
These were shown to be:

- Parents don't approve.
- It might affect schoolwork or sport.
- It's not legal until you are eighteen. The police have the right to stop you, and even take you to the Children's Court if you are found drinking, especially if you behave badly.
- It doesn't taste so good until you get older.
- It's expensive — there are better things to do with your money.

Experimenting with drugs: smoking, and then what else?

'I wish you'd tell him how dangerous it is.' Adam had been found with a group of friends inhaling spray paint and liquid paper in plastic bags. They were in disgrace, but not very repentant. 'Don't go on, Mum, they all do it. I know it's stupid. And it was only this once.'

Adam's mother went on to say that it was not like him to do this. 'If it had been his older sister, I might not have been surprised,' she said. 'But Adam's only twelve. He might have died. And now we feel that we can't trust him.'

The disturbing fact is that more and more young people are experimenting with drugs, and at an earlier and earlier age. They start doing it for all sorts of reasons, but at first it is mostly just to try it out for fun. Parents worry that a relatively less serious drug experimentation may lead to the use of dangerous and addictive drugs later on. But how do you prevent this happening? So far there isn't much evidence that education programmes and public health measures have done much to stop teenagers using drugs.

Do pre-teenagers really use drugs?

There have been several surveys of drug use in Australian school-children. One recent survey of Victorian students showed that by year 7, when most children would be just twelve or thirteen, over 40% have tried alcohol, probably 20% drink regularly, and almost 50% have used cigarettes, about 18% regularly. Although only a few (about 5%) had tried marijuana, almost a quarter of students had tried inhalants. By this age, some students were already trying such drugs as amphetamines, ecstasy and hallucinating drugs such as LSD and narcotics. Except for inhalants, which were mainly a younger teenager's drug, usage of all drugs steadily increased into the teens.

We have always known that many pre-teenagers smoke occasionally, but why would they do something as dangerous as inhaling solvents, glue and other substances, or use drugs, at their age?

Why do pre-teenagers smoke?

Part of the answer to why children use dangerous and illegal drugs might come from our experience with smoking. This has been widely studied and there have been many educational and public health programmes focused on persuading young people not to smoke. We might start by asking why so many pre-teenagers smoke in spite of all the knowledge about the harmful effects of tobacco. Pre-teenagers may not think of smoking cigarettes as using a drug, of course, even though they have probably been taught that tobacco contains harmful substances and that nicotine is a very addictive substance.

A child might start to smoke just to find out what it is like, but continue for social reasons. Even if the pre-teenager doesn't enjoy it much at first, it might make them feel pretty mature, and it might make it easier to join in with other pre-teenagers who also smoke. Even if this doesn't happen, most pre-teenagers will think that everyone has to try it out for themselves some time, and it's better in company.

Pre-teenagers might reason it out this way: *although you know you shouldn't smoke, you also know that everyone tries it out, so it can't be that bad. And anyway, probably your mother or your uncle or your older sister smokes, or they did once, so it can't be a really serious crime. Whether you feel different when you smoke or not, it's a pretty cool thing to do, and it's something to do with friends, especially if your best friend smokes too.*

Parents might not see it this way at all. For them, smoking certainly is not cool. There are plenty of other ways to be part of a group of friends without smoking. Not all pre-teenagers smoke, despite what their child says. Parents feel that children should obey their parents' wishes. They should take notice of the harmful effects of tobacco. Smoking is antisocial and expensive and dirty and objectionable.

Pre-teenagers might think that their way of looking at smoking is more realistic than their parents' way, especially for their own age group. Anyway, they will give it up when they want to (they think).

It's not so much for the drug effect as the social benefit that leads pre-teenagers to smoke. Eventually, of course, they smoke because they enjoy it. Perhaps they enjoy the whole process of sharing a cigarette and lighting up. Perhaps they feel more relaxed with the effect of nicotine. An advantage of smoking (for the smoker who wants to get the drug effect of nicotine) is that the nicotine enters the blood through the lungs very quickly, so the effect is felt very quickly. Unfortunately, if there is a quick response to a drug it makes it much more likely that a child will try it again. Drugs that have a quick effect are more liable to be addictive. That is why most drugs of addiction are smoked, sniffed, inhaled or injected into a vein.

Pre-teenagers often look for new experiences

Smoking cigarettes may be largely a social experience for many pre-teenagers, but things that alter your mind and give you feelings you haven't experienced before are something different. And that is what inhaling (or sniffing) aerosols and solvents and other inhalants do.

It is also more exciting if it is a bit dangerous. Pre-teenagers have plenty of opportunity to learn about sniffing inhalants. They have probably heard about it from older children, or seen something about it on TV, or maybe had a talk about it in lessons at school. It's likely that they do it in groups, and sniffing inhalants are fairly cheap, they are easy to obtain, and it has a very quick effect.

Inhaling volatile substances is dangerous. It is much more serious than smoking. It is dangerous because of the way some children do it. They may spray the aerosol into a plastic bag, and then put it over their mouth to breathe it in. There is a risk that they may lose consciousness and then asphyxiate. This is a special risk for those who inhale when they are by themselves. At least if they are with a friend there is a hope of rescue. The volatile substances themselves are dangerous because they may damage the brain. It is common for people who have sniffed substances in this way to be confused, to lose their memory and to have difficulty in thinking clearly. Although much of their thinking ability will probably return with time, there may actually be permanent damage. Some of the substances that children inhale also damage the liver.

Prevention is always better than cure: but is it easier at this age?

How can you stop pre-teens experimenting with drugs? One thing everyone seems to agree about is that the pre-teens are the time to start protecting our children from drugs if we are to discourage them as teenagers from abusing drugs and harming themselves. For some teenagers it may not really be possible to prevent them using drugs, especially tobacco and alcohol and even marijuana, and the best we can do is to minimise the harm they can cause. Even so, every pre-teen deserves to have the best chance possible to avoid harmful drug use.

What can parents do at this age?

Parents can do a lot at the pre-teen stage. It might get a lot harder to influence them when they are older, so even if you think that your child would never touch drugs, you might consider the fact that he or she will certainly come into contact with drugs and will get to know teenagers who do use drugs. Drug use occurs in all secondary schools. None are exempt, despite firm school rules, harsh punishments and education programmes.

SET A GOOD EXAMPLE THAT YOUR PRE-TEENAGER CAN FOLLOW
There is ample evidence that children of parents who smoke or use other drugs are more likely to do so themselves. It is not enough to say 'Don't smoke like me, look how it has harmed my health, see how I can't give it up now'. Now in fact *is* the time to give up smoking. Pre-teenagers are very much influenced by adult role models, and at their age, parents, especially the same-sex parent, are the most influential role models. They may not always be so during the next few years.

MAKE SURE THAT YOUR PRE-TEENAGER IS WELL INFORMED

You don't have to give lectures on drugs, but it is essential that children are given the facts about drugs as they become interested, and in terms that they can understand and in ways that interest them. As parents, you can at least get into the habit of discussing drugs while your pre-teen is interested in your viewpoint and respects your advice.

Unfortunately, group discussions at school sometimes have the opposite effect that is intended. Sometimes class discussions about drugs seem to excite the children and make them want to try them out for themselves. There are good school programmes of course, but there is not much evidence that this form of education actually stops teenagers using drugs.

(See page 185 for further discussions on drugs and their effects.)

HELP YOUR PRE-TEENAGER DEVELOP STRENGTHS AND STRATEGIES TO RESIST TEMPTATION TO USE DRUGS

It isn't always easy for a pre-teenager to resist trying out a forbidden experience like inhaling or smoking or drinking (or other exciting things that they think might make them feel good). Look at it from their viewpoint. *It might be very hard if you don't just try it out, especially if your best friends want you to do it with them. If you don't join in, you might feel really left out, or you might feel a bit of a woos. You might get teased for being scared to try. You might even be bullied into it. Worst of all, you might lose your friends.*

Work on the positive ways of saying no. Your pre-teenager probably isn't the only one who may feel pressured at times into trying out things, including drugs, that they don't want to do. Suggest they talk it out with a really good friend: it will be easier if two or three in the group say no to drugs. No-one wants to be the odd one out.

Help them to think of good reasons for not using drugs. 'I'd be interested, but my sports coach won't let us.' 'Thanks, but I'm in training, so I better not.' 'I can't. I've got an important match on at the weekend.' 'I tried it once or twice, but it didn't do anything for me.' Sometimes the old 'My parents would kill me' is as good a response as any at this age. Probably the best reply of all is a firm 'No. I'm not interested'. But this isn't always easy for pre-teenagers who aren't very sure of themselves and their place in the social group.

GIVE YOUR CHILD LOTS OF RESPECT, AND HELP BUILD THEIR SELF-ESTEEM, SO THAT THEY DON'T NEED DRUGS TO BOOST SELF-CONFIDENCE OR MAINTAIN FRIENDSHIPS

Studies on teenagers who abuse drugs have shown that those with low self-esteem may be more likely to use drugs than those with high self-esteem and plenty of self-confidence. Work on their self-confidence and feelings of being respected.

(See page 54 for a discussion on self-esteem.)

MAKE SURE YOU ARE AWARE IF THERE ARE THINGS TROUBLING YOUR PRE-TEENAGER

Some teenagers use drugs, especially marijuana, as a way to feel happier and cope with depression and unhappiness. There are much better ways of feeling happier than being in a drugged state, even though the dreamy high of inhalants or the happy peace of marijuana may seem at the time to feel good. Take time to get to know your pre-teenager, and to listen to their worries and upsets. Don't assume that life for a pre-teenager is always a ball.

CONCENTRATE ON THE POSITIVE ASPECTS OF A DRUG-FREE BODY

People who don't use drugs are fitter, stronger, look more alert and alive and get the things done that they want to do. Focus on these aspects of health. Pre-teenagers like to have an attractive fit body (like any other age) but they need to work on it (like any other age).

TEAM UP WITH OTHER PARENTS TO PRESENT A UNITED FRONT
ON DRUGS
Any efforts you make as a parent will be more effective if other
parents take the same stance, particularly if you think there might
be a drug problem at your pre-teenager's school or in the
neighbourhood. It is good for parents to talk about their
common concerns for their children, but many parents don't
consider there are problems for their pre-teenage child, and might
miss the opportunity to discuss the topic of prevention of
problems at this age.

Sadness and depression

*'I'm no good.' Ten-year-old Ken had said this after another row
with his father about his behaviour. Ken's mother wondered about
his self-esteem, and why he didn't seem to care much about things
recently. When he glumly announced that he was no good at
anything, and flung down his bat during a game of backyard cricket,
his mother thought it was time to look into what was going wrong for
him. He seemed so sad these days.*

Most people think that pre-teens are usually happy, and so they are.
But not all, and many disguise their unhappiness in various ways such
as bad behaviour, not trying at school or games or just saying that
they are no good. Pre-teens can get quite depressed, but it isn't
always the same sort of depression as adults, and it usually isn't so
obvious. They almost certainly won't tell you that they are depressed,
and probably wouldn't really understand what being depressed meant
anyway. They may feel so bad about themselves that parents and
teachers might suspect that the problem is one of poor self-esteem.

Low self-esteem and depression have a lot in common. In
both cases children feel that they aren't much good at anything,
that they are pretty worthless. Low self-esteem, however, is

often pretty well entrenched and present for some time; whereas childhood depression may be fairly recent, and even children with good self-esteem can get depressed. In both cases, children can feel rather hopeless. They may feel it's not worth trying, maybe because they won't succeed (if self-esteem is low), or because who cares anyway? They may drop out of social activities or stop trying at school for the same reasons. 'Who'd want me to play with them?' 'My teacher doesn't like me.' 'I don't care.' Often when children say they don't care, they mean that they care a lot, but it hurts to care, and it helps if you pretend that you don't.

Although self-esteem and depression have quite a lot in common it is better to distinguish them because the strategies that help one may not always be so helpful for the other. On the other hand, once the cause of a child's sadness and depression is understood, it will help them to feel better about themselves. Raising self-esteem becomes the next step to recovery.

How do you tell if a pre-teen is depressed?

Parents can tell when their child is sad. But the sadness may be due to obvious and quite understandable reasons, such as death of a loved relative, the loss of a friend at school, the break-up of their parents' marriage. The death of a pet can be overwhelming for a pre-teen.

But sadness and depression are not quite the same. Children who are depressed often withdraw from those around them, including their family. They may feel so bad that they feel it's all their own fault that they feel that way. They may *feel* so bad that they *act* bad. When a pre-teen acts badly, parents may feel that they need to discipline their child. They don't get to know the real reason why their child acted badly, especially if there wasn't much of an obvious reason for it. This of course may make the pre-teen feel even worse, and more depressed.

They may be confused about their emotions, and find it very hard to tell their parents how they feel. Child psychiatrists sometimes need to use special ways to help a child express depression, such as through drawings or stories or play, in order to understand how they really feel. No wonder parents sometimes find it difficult to work out what is the trouble with their child.

Depressed pre-teens often lose their appetite, even for foods they usually like. They may lose weight. They may have difficulty sleeping. They may get bad grades at school, but not seem to care. They may lack enthusiasm for things they used to enjoy, such as family outings or visits from friends. They may sulk more often, or go to their room by themselves, especially if there has been a fight with their siblings. They are more likely to get headaches or stomach pains.

What can parents do if they think that their pre-teen may be depressed?

Often all that is needed is to spend time with them, just one or other parent without the rest of the family. It can help to listen to them, even if it takes quite a long time for them to start telling you how they feel. Perhaps grandparents or an older sibling may find time to sit and listen. It is important to take their misery seriously, and not just laugh it off, or tell them that they will get over it (they will, but perhaps not without a lot of help). You may feel that there isn't really a good enough reason for them to be depressed, and in this case you should realise that sometimes it needs experienced help to sort it out.

If you feel that your pre-teen may be depressed but you don't seem able to help them, consider asking for advice professionally. This may be something that a child psychiatrist or psychologist can help with. Talk it over with your family doctor.

What about encouraging signs?

There are many ways that a pre-teen can tell you that they are not depressed, or that they are feeling better. They may of course act happy, and laugh (but don't be deceived by smiles; they sometimes hide real misery). They may start to tell you interesting things that they have done, or funny things they have seen. They may start taking an interest in things around them or on television, and ask questions and suggest answers. They may boast a little about themselves (encourage them). They might start eating well, and going to sleep easily. They may have peaceful nights, and get up in the morning looking reasonably cheerful. They might ask a friend around after school.

Ken did need help. He felt no-one understood him. He felt rejected by his father, who in fact wanted to help but thought that Ken should be trying harder, and not just give up. He felt that his mother was too busy with his younger sisters to listen to him. When he tried to talk to her, she always said 'Tell me afterwards', and then forgot all about him. Even his teacher at school lost patience with the way he seldom bothered to contribute to class discussion.

However, he was able to talk to a counsellor recommended by their family doctor, and felt better when he knew that everyone was really taking his difficulties seriously. When his parents realised how he felt, they started to spend time just with him.

It only needed a few minutes a day, but things started to improve for Ken.

Family breakdown

Tania was now ten and had a health problem that needed regular medical treatment if she was to avoid serious problems in later life. It had been inherited from her father, and this fact hadn't made relations between her parents any better, as they were having marital problems of their own, and finding that their daughter had a chronic health problem made things worse. Her mother's family didn't help when they hinted that ill health didn't come from their side of the family.

The growing disharmony was pretty obvious during the medical visits. Both parents came with her, and they contradicted each rather often when telling me about Tania. Tania was responding by refusing to take her medication and becoming very clinging to her parents.

Finally, the parents separated. It wasn't a very comfortable arrangement for either of them as they contested custody arrangements. Instead of coming together, they took it in turns to come in to see me with Tania, and much of the consultation was directed at the other parent's faults and potentially dangerous parenting styles, rather than focusing on Tania's own health. One thing was clear, however: they both loved Tania dearly and wanted the best for her. It was just that their own personal problems were preoccupying them. As this continued, Tania's distress became more obvious.

More than one in four marriages end in separation or divorce. The break-up often happens when there are still dependent children in their rather vulnerable pre-teens. It is almost impossible to shield older children from the disharmony and arguments that usually lead up to separation, and which may continue long afterwards. Often parents are so angry with each other that they find it hard to put their children's interests first, no matter how good their intentions.

There are three periods that are critical for the children during the process of family break-up

1. THE DISHARMONY AND UNHAPPINESS THAT PRECEDES SEPARATION
Parents usually try hard not to involve their children in the arguments and fights that may take place over years before the marriage partnership finally breaks down. They may agree never to argue in front of the children. They may put on a brave front

when they are together with the children. They may be successful in this, but usually pre-teenagers become very aware of their parents' difficulties. If they were not aware that the relationship was under threat, and not prepared for what may follow, a decision to separate can be devastating. It can be very like an unexpected death in the family.

Almost all parents have arguments and some parents seem unable to agree on almost anything, especially on how to bring up their children. Most families have fights sometimes, some more than others of course. Sometimes the fault is mostly on one side, but often both contribute. Very young children are upset when their parents fight, but when they reach the pre-teens, they start to question family relationships and the role of their parents. Many will have friends whose parents have separated, and they may be starting to become aware of the frailty of families by watching the soapies on television. They know that some parents split up, but surely not their mother and father?

I sometimes ask teenagers who have been involved in family conflict when it was that they first realised that adults (including their parents) are not perfect and are capable of making mistakes just like grown-up children. They almost always say that it was in the years before their teens. Until then they were convinced that their parents were faultless. It can come as a shock to find out that parents are not perfect, and can make terrible mistakes in their relationship with each other. How are the mighty fallen!

It may not occur to pre-teenage children that the rows and arguments will lead to family breakdown. However upsetting it is to see and hear their mother and father arguing and fighting, it is as nothing compared with the blow of separation. When they are a little older they may see family rows and disharmony in a different light, and may even encourage one or other parent to leave. They are much more likely to judge their parents, and may take sides and come to think that separation will make life better for everyone.

Not so the pre-teenager, who usually wants above all for the family to stay intact (except for an older brother or sister perhaps, who is a bossy pain and whose bedroom and computer might become theirs if they left home). The exceptions are when there is a lot of frightening physical violence, or drunkenness or if the pre-teenager has been abused physically or sexually. Even then, separation will probably lead to great emotional turmoil. Pre-teenagers might think it was their fault that their parents fight. After all, many of their arguments were about the children. Why can't their parents just settle down and be friends? Why can't they just stop fighting? They expect the children to stop and make up when they are fighting, don't they?

Pre-teenagers, who are just starting to get some insight into personal relationships and the frailty of adults of both sexes, need a lot of support when their parents' marriage seems to be failing.

They need to be reassured that both their parents do love them, even though love between each other is heavily strained.

They may need to be told it isn't their fault that the family is under threat.

They need to be reassured about things that will still be there even if their parents can't stay together — the family home, the family pet, school, doing things together, the grandparents.

If these things are also under threat it will be harder for the pre-teenager. The family house is likely to be important, because it is familiar and 'home'. Family pets may be very much loved and a continuing part of their life. The threat of changing school and losing school friends may greatly increase the distress for the pre-teenager if it happens at the same time that they are losing one or other parent. All this should be talked through with the children, especially pre-teenagers and teenagers, as separation approaches.

Grandparents sometimes may be able to help by providing continuity in the family, and can often talk to their grandchildren quietly about the difficulties for their parents, provided they avoid blaming them. Not that the parents will always want them to do so, especially if one or other grandparent takes sides in the marriage breakdown.

There is a lot that parents can do to prepare their children if the marriage is under threat and separation seems inevitable. Most of what is needed requires talking about the situation, reassuring them about what will stay the same and preparing them for what will be different.

2. THE SEPARATION

Most pre-teenagers are deeply upset when their parents separate. Some studies on broken families have suggested that it has been the preceding rows and fights that have caused all the distress, and that the separation actually made things better for the children. Of course, that is what parents take into account when they do decide to break up.

However, not all studies agree with this. As far as the children are concerned, separation is seldom their idea of a solution. An argumentative mother or an aggressive father who fight but live together may be much better than the loss of one or other parent. Sometimes the break-up makes the situation much worse for the pre-teenager who has reached the age of understanding what is happening, but is not at the stage of mature insight into complex human personal relationships.

At the time of separation and divorce, parents are often resentful and confrontational, especially when it comes to custody of the children and financial arrangements. Even though there may be opportunities for counselling the children at that time, it is highly stressful for them just as it is for their parents. They should certainly be given the opportunity for professional counselling if they appear confused or distressed.

When the pre-teenager has to make a decision about which parent he or she wants to live with, it is an extra burden of responsibility. Often there is no doubt in their minds: they want to stay with Mum or they are going with Dad. But what if one child wants to be with one parent, and another wants to go with the other? This means separating from a sibling as well. Sometimes they can't decide, and the question of friends and school influences their decision. Sometimes they feel that one or the other parent would be very lonely without them and they should stay with them Often it isn't practical to stay with their father, even if they badly wanted to.

Often when the pre-teenager does decide to live with one parent, the other may be hurt and resentful. This is very likely if a boy decides to live with his father, while his mother believes that it was the father who caused the marriage breakdown and who had taken little responsibility for early child care. It would then be very difficult for his mother to disguise her resentment from her pre-teenager. I have several times heard a mother say, in this situation 'I feel that I no longer have a son', so hurt has she been at his apparent rejection of her. But to lose his mother and her love is usually the last thing that the pre-teenager wants, wherever he lives, and his mother's distress adds to his own.

3. AFTER THE SEPARATION

Things may take a few months to settle down. Don't expect rapid adjustment to new family arrangements unless the preparation for separation has been very good. Sometimes pre-teenagers who have lost a parent through separation go through a normal process of grieving very like what happens after the death of someone they love. The process tends to go through stages.

There may be disbelief and denial.

Surely their parents will come to their senses soon and Dad will return? He has just gone away for a bit.

They may be angry.

Why did their parents do it? Whose fault was it? They may refuse to see or talk to one or other parent, blaming them for everything. Anger and blame and guilt all go together. This may lead to bad behaviour, crying, aggression, sleep disturbance or difficulties at school.

Sadness and anger often go together in the pre-teens

They miss the good times the family had together. They miss their absent father. Seeing him at weekends may even make it seem worse as it reminds them of when they were together as a family. The access meetings with him may be difficult. Should they just pretend that it is part of family life? Should it be some sort of special outing? Either way it may be unsettling for both father and children.

The sadness and resentment may go on and on, even when custody arrangements are in place and seem to be working. It will be much worse if access arrangements are under dispute, or if one parent does not trust the other during access or actively prevents it.

Eventually children adjust to the new arrangements. Sooner or later they get to accept that their parents don't live together any more. That doesn't mean to say that they don't secretly hope that one day their parents will reunite. This is often fantasy, and as the pre-teenager moves into their teens, so their understanding and acknowledgment of reality will help them realise this is impossible.

There are a number of things that parents can do, and some things to avoid, to help this adjustment process go smoothly

THE SEPARATED PARENT SHOULD TRY TO KEEP IN CONTACT
If there are access arrangements that allow regular visits, make sure that your work and personal life allow for this. In any case, don't forget birthdays, Christmas and other special occasions. Regular phone calls, letters and cards help to show that you are still interested. Ask about how they are going at school and sport, and what they are doing for fun. Tell them about yourself and what you are doing. Make them feel that you are still connected. However hurt you may feel about the situation and the loss of your children, keep in touch. It's well

worthwhile, even if at times they don't respond or don't seem to welcome the contacts. Attitudes change, and it will make it easier later when reconciliation between estranged parent and teenager or young adult can occur.

DON'T SPOIL ACCESS ARRANGEMENTS

Sometimes the parent who has custody and cares for the pre-teenager feels so angry with their ex-spouse that they tend to sabotage access arrangements. They may feel that the contact is not good for the child, or that the other parent doesn't deserve to see the children. Sometimes they are concerned about how upset the pre-teenager seemed after the last visit, and don't want this to be repeated. Sometimes a child will say 'Do I really have to go?' If they say 'Yes', it might sound like a punishment to endure. If they say 'No', it may not really be in the child's best interests in the long run.

There are lots of subtle ways that access can be spoiled for the pre-teenager:

- by making attractive arrangements that clash with access times and which the child will have to miss
- by saying derogatory things about the other parent (however much they are deserved)
- by suggesting that the child has a cold and is too sick to go
- by suggesting that the child doesn't want to go, or refuses to go
- by never having them ready on time
- by constantly finding that the access times interfere with important things like a homework assignment or parties and sport
- by complaining to everyone how washed out and grumpy the children are after seeing the other parent
- by criticising what they did together or what they were fed: 'Not McDonalds again?'

The scope is almost endless, but the effect is the same. It won't help the pre-teenager to adjust to a split family, or to feel happier with an absent parent, and it might backfire later in the teenage years when different arrangements might be needed.

DON'T USE THE PRE-TEENAGER TO CHECK UP ON THE OTHER PARENT

Try not to ask, however subtly, whether there is a new partner around, or what they are doing together. You can ask about the absent parent in an interested and perhaps caring way, but not with a view to criticism. 'How is your Dad?' is fine, but 'Is he still drinking heavily?' is not. 'Did Vera go with you?' may be OK, but 'Is his girlfriend still hanging around?' certainly is not. Anything that sounds as if you are checking up with a view to criticism is unhelpful to your pre-teenager, however much it might seem to help you.

TRY NOT TO SAY BAD THINGS ABOUT THE OTHER PARENT

However badly your ex-spouse behaved towards the family and during the marriage breakdown, it is usually harmful to dwell on the bad times when talking to your pre-teenager. They will probably have a pretty good idea of what went on anyway, and may be struggling to find some good things to help them feel better about each parent. They almost certainly still love each of their parents, however much they say they don't, or however angry they may be about what they have done. They don't really want to hear more bad things about someone they love. It could even make them feel bitter towards you. *'Mum goes on and on about Dad. He's not really like that at all.'*

Everyone has some good points, even an ex-spouse. They must have or you wouldn't have lived with them in the first place. There must have been some good times together. Try to recall them when you are talking to your pre-teenager about their other parent.

*TRY NOT TO RELY ON YOUR PRE-TEENAGER TO SUPPLY THE
SUPPORT AND COMPANIONSHIP YOU LOST WHEN THE MARRIAGE
BROKE DOWN*

Few parents would consciously use their pre-teenager this way,
but it often does work out like this. Naturally a single supporting
mother (or father) will need help around the house, and that
responsibility is good for the pre-teenager. Naturally the older
children may need to grow up rather quickly if they suddenly
seem to be 'the man of the house' or 'my right-hand person'.

There are two dangers that could result. The first is that it
may interfere with the necessary developmental process of puberty
in which increasing independence from parents and strengthening
social links with their own age group become so necessary. The
second can happen if you start a new relationship, and particularly
if a new partner comes into your home. Then the pre-teenager
(who might be a teenager by now), could feel they have been
pushed aside in their role of support and companionship by
the new partner. It could even make them sabotage the new
relationship by being nasty and uncooperative with the
new partner. Teenagers have a powerful ability to interfere
with new partnerships just at the time when they are preparing to
move away from the family circle, and just at the time that their
parent may most need to look to their own future happiness.

*GIVE LOTS OF REASSURANCE TO YOUR PRE-TEENAGER IF YOU
ARE EMBARKING ON A NEW RELATIONSHIP*

Children who have gone through one family disruption may
feel very insecure about losing their remaining parent. The loss
may be one of having to share their mother's or father's love
with another person, especially someone the pre-teenager
didn't pick and may not like. It still is a disruption in the family
for them, and they may feel less important to you. Of course,
they may really like the new partner and be pleased that their
parent is so much happier now than when they were alone.

AVOID BRIBERY TO GAIN APPROVAL

It is not helpful to the pre-teenager, or a child at any age, to be seduced by offers of expensive presents or exotic trips and holidays. It is particularly difficult if one parent is very well off financially while the other is not. Either way, bribery hurts the child's relationship with both parents, however much they want the presents or money or trips. It is always better if both parents discuss together what things should be given to the child. Even if the present can't come from both of them, at least it is by their mutual agreement, just as it probably would have been if the parents had stayed together. Perhaps each parent could make a contribution if it was for something like an expensive computer they needed for schoolwork, even if one parent gave much more than the other.

A NEW PARTNER CAN'T REPLACE AN ABSENT PARENT

In time, of course, a step-parent becomes a very important part of a child's life. But they can seldom replace a natural parent, especially if that parent is still around and trying to maintain their relationship with their son or daughter. It is helpful if the new partner tries to show interest in their stepchildren, and talks to them and does things with them that they would like. They should be careful, however, not to fall into the traps that await any new partner in the life of a pre-teenager. They will be quick to criticise and find fault, and will resent it if they try to take over the role of their real father or mother.

If the pre-teenager chooses to call their step-parent Mum or Dad, that's fine. Otherwise using their first name is best, so that the relationship with the absent parent isn't forgotten or devalued. It is a mistake for the new partner to expect too much from the stepchildren. Affection and respect come slowly, and have to be earned. It's nice if the pre-teenager says that they have two fathers, and recognises each of them and the place they have in their lives. But this may take time and should not be forced on a child at this age.

Even when everyone, including the pre-teenager, is trying hard to make the new arrangements work after a family breakdown and changing relationships, things can go wrong. Sometimes it is wise to seek some professional help when this seems to be happening.

With time and patience, however, most changing family arrangements work out fine and children make the necessary adjustments. Pre-teenagers are usually resilient and learn to cope with their life.

THE NEW PARTNER SHOULD BE VERY RELUCTANT TO DISCIPLINE STEPCHILDREN

They should be cautious about taking part in their upbringing at all. At pre-teenage they will almost certainly resent it and may never forgive it. It is hard to resist helping out when a child is being very trying to their mother and clearly needs a short sharp rebuke. But the pre-teenager will probably say 'You're not my father' and this will lead to further upsets. A parent needs support from their new partner but it should be one step removed from the firing line.

It was interesting to see how Tania eventually coped with her parents' marriage breakdown. After they had been to the Family Law Court and custody was granted jointly, and arrangements were in place for Tania to live with her mother but to spend a lot of time with her father, everything settled down well. Both parents would once again come with Tania for her regular checkups, but now they would talk with each other about the things they were doing to help her, and there was no more trouble about Tania not taking her medication.

Next stop, teenage

Teenagers may have a bad reputation for giving their parents a hard time, but for most families the teenage years are fun. It certainly is never boring or dull.

The years leading up to the teens give parents a chance to make sure that adolescence is a good time for their children. Not all the time of course. They will make mistakes, sometimes spectacular ones. Making mistakes is one way to learn, and it's probably the best way, provided they don't suffer too much. But a little bit of pain is good for them sometimes. Parents can't protect their children from all of life's problems in the teenage years.

So you have brought them this far, right up to their teens. You have prepared them for the years ahead. If there were any problems that threatened their successful passage through puberty, you have identified them and resolved them. You have given them every chance for a successful transition to adult life.

Now you can sit back and look forward to the fun times ahead, when your children explore their teenage world and expand their minds and develop their abilities and start to achieve their potential as adults. They might even allow you to share some of these excitements with them.

I remember a twelve-year-old girl telling me the advice she got from an older sister when she asked her what it was like going through adolescence. Everyone had told her it would be hard.
'Not really,' her sister had said. 'Actually, it just happened. You kind of look at yourself from time to time and say "Oh, look at that – that's interesting", but it's no big deal, and mostly you are too busy getting on with your life to think about the big worries that your parents seem to have.'

Suggestions for further reading

Coil, Carolyn, *Becoming an achiever – a student guide,* Hawker
   Brownlow Education, Melbourne, 1994.
Coil, Carolyn, *Motivating underachievers – 172 strategies for success,*
   Hawker Brownlow Education, Melbourne, 1994.
   (Carolyn Coil's books include practical and inventive
   suggestions for motivating students.)
Court, John, *You and your teenager,* Angus & Robertson,
   Australia, 1995.
   (This book discusses teenagers, how to understand them and
   how to live with them.)
Mellor, Andrew, *Bullying and how to fight it: a guide for families,*
   Scottish Council for Research in Education, 1993.
   (A booklet providing practical advice on how families and
   schools can tackle the problem of bullying in schools.)
Wallace, Ian, *You and your ADD child,* HarperCollins*Publishers,*
   Australia, 1996.
   (Ian Wallace's book provides practical strategies for parents to
   cope with a child who has ADD.)
Webber, Ruth, *Split Ends,* ACER. Melbourne, 1996.
   (A book to help teenagers understand broken families and
   cope with stepfamilies.)

All of these books are currently available in Australia.

index